W. H. Kent

A Historical Review of the Causes and Issues

that led to the overthrow of the Republican Party in Kansas in 1892 -

including a history of the exciting events of the legislative embroglio and

its final settlement

W. H. Kent

A Historical Review of the Causes and Issues
that led to the overthrow of the Republican Party in Kansas in 1892 - including a history of the exciting events of the legislative embroglio and its final settlement

ISBN/EAN: 9783337390495

Printed in Europe, USA, Canada, Australia, Japan

Cover: Foto ©Andreas Hilbeck / pixelio.de

More available books at **www.hansebooks.com**

HISTORICAL REVIEW

OF THE

CAUSES AND ISSUES

THAT LED TO THE

OVERTHROW OF THE REPUBLICAN PARTY

IN KANSAS IN 1892.

Including a History of the Exciting Events of the Legislative Embroglio and its Final Settlement, in which Bloodshed and Internecine War were Narrowly Averted.

BY W. H. KENT.

PUBLISHED BY
THE TOPEKA DAILY PRESS 1893.

A HISTORICAL REVIEW

OF THE

CAUSES AND ISSUES

THAT LED TO THE

OVERTHROW OF THE REPUBLICAN PARTY

IN KANSAS 1892.

THE UNHOLY ALLIANCE.

THE COMMON INTERESTS OF THE CORPORA-
TIONS OFFICIALLY ESPOUSED BY THE REPUB-
LICAN PARTY.—"THE RAILROAD QUESTION
IN AMERICA IS LIKE THE IRISH LAND QUES-
TION."

The history of Kansas, from the pen of a
second Macauley, who may, perhaps, be
born in the Twentieth Century, will be
among the classics of the future.

It will no longer be necessary to return to
the days of Cæsar, of Cataline, or of Han-
nibal the Suffete, to find examples of un-
dled ambition, of grinding oppression
tyranny, of the arrogance of a plutoc-
and the use of mercenaries to enslave
eople, of conspiracy and its final over-

will be in the volume thus written

by the impartial Historian no chapter more
thrilling, nor one read with greater interest,
wonder and curiosity, than that which sha
faithfully portray the events which have occurred during the past decade, and more especially the last year. These led up to the
final overthrow of the Republican party, after an almost uninterrupted and absolute
domination that was marked by the perpe-
tration of every crime in the political calen-
dar, in the name of Republicanism; whose
motto, literally construed, has been: "Liberty means License."

The once proud Republican party is no
longer the Republican party save in name
but has discarded the principles of Lincoln
and other great founders and leaders in the
cause of freedom and equal rights, to bend
the knee to the corporations, and lend willing obedience to the edicts of the money

kings issued from their palaces on Wall street, a section of New York that is smaller than any little German principality or dukedom, yet which has been, for a quarter of a century, by the grace of the Republican party, the financial center of the Republic, and its money princes the absolute masters of the banking system of the whole country and of the Nation's credit.

At the seventeenth convention of the American Bankers' Association, held at New Orleans November 11 and 12, 1891, the president, introducing Prof. Arthur T. Hadley, of Yale college, who had been invited to prepare a paper to be read before the convention on the subject: "Recent Railroad Legislation and Its Effect Upon the Finances of the United States," said:

GENTLEMEN—We are all so largely interested in railroads and railroad securities that I take great pleasure in introducing to you Prof. Arthur T. Hadley, of Yale college, who has made this the subject of profound study.

Of the remarkable statements made by Prof. Hadley, the Bankers' Magazine and Statistical Journal of December, 1891, quotes the following:

Whatever causes shrinkage in railroad values is of importance to a body of financiers, because railroad securities are more important than any other line of investments and properties, more than all others put together. A loss of 1 per cent. in interest on railroad securities would mean a fall in capital valuation greater than the whole wheat and cotton crop of the country put together.

If we look at the systems immediately west of Chicago, we find that since the passage of the interstate commerce law, they have shrunk in value $60,000,000, or more than 25 per cent. of the par value of their stocks.

Such a fall can only have been due to legislative action. The interstate commerce law, which had been supposed to be the end of a struggle for railroad control, was only the beginning.

The individual states went further and did a great many things with far less wisdom than the interstate commerce commission. Finally the prohibition of pools prevented the railroads from taking measures in self defense.

The railroad question in America is like the Irish land question. Railroads are owned in the east and operated in the west, just as the Irish land is owned in England, and there is an effort on the part of the people who use the property to fix the rates, instead of letting it be done by the people who own it.

It is not likely that this effort will succeed.

A ... ation of hostilities will result in the disastrous experiment of taking the control of railroads from invested capital.

Here, then, is the admission of the union and close relationship of the banks and the railroads; of the fact that a struggle has begun for the regulation of railroad rates, which has as yet only reached the incipient stage that pools are indispensable to the maintainance of extortionate rates; that the continuation of restrictive legislation will result in government control, and finally that the railroad question in America is like the Irish land question.

So many wholesome truths from so high an authority on the subject, the opposition could scarcely have dared to expect.

The views of Prof. Hadley as endorsed by the Bankers' Association were those already adopted by the Republican party, and now freshly enunciated, and henceforth the twin corporations became more than ever the objects of tenderest solicitude.

THE PARTY OF JUDAS.

THE REPUBLICANS BETRAY THE PEOPLE AND ESPOUSE THE CAUSE OF THE CORPORATIONS. —THE CRUCIAL TEST.—THE ONLY ALTERNATIVE.

In this crisis there was no alternative but for the people to organize and equip themselves for a struggle but just commenced, and aptly compared to that between the English lords and their Irish tenantry.

The Republican party had always been peculiarly zealous in providing for the system of railroads west of the Missouri river, and known as the Pacific railroads. The National congress, then Republican, had enriched the corporations by enormous grants of land from the public domain, while State and Territorial Legislatures vied with each other in enlarging corporate privileges, and adding to their franchises.

In Kansas, Nebraska, Wyoming and C rado the railway managers became crats, and were permitted to dictate own terms. They named United States Senators, Governors, Legislators, Mayors and Councilmen. State constitutions, Legislative enactments and City ordinances were drafted at the general offices, approved by the Directory, and immediately passed by the subservient tools the Republicans elected. The vast territory that was quickly spanned by the new lines was peopled with a rapidity that has had no equal since mankind was introduced into the Garden of Eden, and the home seekers and settlers who came West to enjoy greater liberty and wider privileges, found themselves reduced to the level of peons, paying tribute to their masters in the shape of annual installments on their lands, for which the railroad companies paid nothing, and which the settlers purchased at almost equal prices prevailing in older states.

The hardship of these brave settlers, the deprivation and destitution which they so patiently bore, their struggles with the elements, with drought and the devastation of grasshoppers, are all matters of history with which every intelligent man, woman and child west of the Missouri river has been familiarized by bitter experience. And in no section of the Trans-Missouri empire has the experience been more bitter than in our grand commonwealth.

The necessities of the case resulting from the untoward circumstances incident to the settlement of a new country forced the people to seek assistance not only for immediate support but for the further development of their new homes.

Financial aid was forthcoming, prompted by the unexampled liberality of the national and state governments to the railroad corporations. The money lenders of the congested New England States saw in the rapid development and settlement of the New West an opportunity to offer the financial aid the settlers sought and demand for their money exacting and usurious interest. The result was the establishment of the loan agent in nearly every village and hamlet in the great West. Under the alluring influence of the new life that appeared to spring up on the prairies and with the mirage of vast rural possessions before their constant gaze the settlers availed themselves of the easy opportunities to obtain ready money

by mortgaging their farms on long time though fabulous rates of interest were demanded for "the accommodation." The result was that mortgages were "plastered" on a large percentage of the tillable acres of the Western States, and particularly of Kansas.

This was the crucial time and test of government—the time when it was easy to discern whether the political party then dominant in the state and country succumbed to the influence of the great corporations and the money power, both of which, octopus like, were fastening their grasp upon the people, or whether the government, through the party, would rise supreme in its majesty and extend its guarding hand over the great army of its subjects toiling to make the desert blossom and rear on the central plain of our grand federation of states a monument to the greatness and benignity of our cherished institution of self-government.

The Republican party had been in power since the great civil war, in which it achieved its renown, and upon which it based its claim to the generous endorsement of the nation. Blinded by the halo of its glory the people trusted and obeyed its mandates, oblivious of the insiduous and subtle influence that was fast gaining control of the machinery of the organization, and which intended, and finally accomplished, the enslavement of the too confiding masses.

It was at this crisis that the Republican party, as a political organization found upon the principles of its early lead ceased to exist except in name only, and came the party of corporate greed and power. Its long continuance in power emboldened its leaders to believe that they had a life tenure of office, and every year increased their arrogance and the burdens inflicted upon the people. They had become pliant tools of corporations, and as this effaced the last lingering trace of honor and conscience, they sank deeper and deeper into the mire of corruption and degradation. So long as they could satisfy the demands of corporation managers, to whom they owed their continuation in power, they forgot the needs of the struggling masses and allow nothing to stand in the way of their self aggrandizement. They were blind to t. Nemesis that was fast overtaking them, an in their desire to perpetuate their power at last were guilty of of outrages which brought swift retribution and destroyed Republican supremacy root and branch.

═══

THE CAMPAIGN AND THE CONTEST.

"CARRYING THE WAR INTO AFRICA." — THE WICHITA TICKET NOMINATED. — THE FOUR STATE CONVENTIONS — VICTORY FOR THE PEOPLE.

As the Republican party, gradually at first but finally swiftfully and shamelessly, arrayed itself as the champion of the money kings, the people entrenched themselves more firmly for the struggle that was inevitable. When the campaign of 1892 opened t found the opposition to corporation tyranny splendidly organized. It was like the o d story of the field planted with dragons' t ~eth, from each of which there sprang forth a knight, full panoplied and ready for battle. Of course the republican papers were keeping up a continual fire on their opponents all along the line, but this time it had not the effect even of causing dismay, much l ess destruction in the ranks of the reform forces. Nor was the unexpected strength of he people developed in merely a single state, but like wildfire, it spread across the iries and the mountains, and found no onsiderable foothold on eastern and southern soil.

The leaders laid their plans well, and in the contest that followed did not stand on the defensive but carried the war into Africa with a vengeance. When the Wichita convention met on June 15, it was with a well-defined and single purpose. The Republican press in treating of the matter at the end of the first day's session contained such headlines as these: "Fusion"—"The People's Party State Convention Thoroughly Under Control of the Fixers"—"Pandemonium Rivalled."—"The Convention a Howling Mob, Beyond Control of Any Reasoning Power," etc., etc.

To show how clearly they reckoned without their host, the same paper, on the morning following, displayed among its headlines these: "Downed"—"The Fusionists Relegated to Back Seats in the People's Party Convention"—"An Ex-Confederate Nominated and the Bloody Chasm Bridged by Patriotism"—"An Old Soldier gets Second Place on the Ticket as a Bid for Veterans."

As a matter of fact, and of history, the Wichita convention, which remained in session two days, and which placed in nomination a straight People's party ticket, was one of the most harmonious ever assembled in the state. The platform was so broad, so comprehensive and so just to all classes that the Republican convention a little later, with a flourish of virtue and fairness, practically endorsed it by adopting almost every plank, with a very weak attempt to conceal the theft.

When Col. W. A. Harris was placed in nomination for Congressman at-Large, his nomination was seconded by 274 ex-union soldiers, a majority of the convention, and that body, having completed its work, adjourned amid the wildest enthusiasm and inspired with an abiding faith that a great victory would be won in the Ides of November.

The following was the ticket nominated at Wichita by the People's party on June 15, 1892:

For Governor—Hon L. D. Lewelling, of Sedgwick county.

For Lieutenant Governor—Col. Percy Daniels, of Crawford county.

For Secretary of State—Capt. R. S. Osborn, of Rooks county.

For Attorney General—Judge John T. Little, of Johnson county.

For Auditor of State—Mr. Van B. Prather, of Cherokee county.

For State Treasurer—Mr. W. H. Biddle, of Butler county.

For Superintendent of Public Instruction —Prof. H. N. Gaines, of Saline county.

For Congressman-at-Large—Col. W. A. Harris, of Leavenworth county.

How different was the gathering of Republicans in Representative hall, at Topeka, on June 30! Flushed by an almost unbroken series of victories extending back for a quarter of a century and confident that, backed by the railroads and the other corporations of the state, the nominees of the convention would be elected with little or no trouble, there was a bitter struggle for place, and enmities were engendered on every side. The state house ring, which never failed to play into the hands of the railroads, and with the whole machinery of state at their command, made a hard fight, but an "up hill one" this time. The more conservative element of the party had really begun to appreciate the strength of the cry. that was going up from all over the state against the tyranny and iniquity of "the gang," and a desperate attempt was made to tone things down to respectability.

This element was successful only to the extent of compelling an unwilling endorsement of many of the principles enunciated by the Wichita convention, which was accomplished after a stubborn and protracted fight.

In the make-up of the ticket the convention could not so easily be controlled, and still under the impression that a nomination here was equivalent to election, rival candidates fought and scrambled and hooted or cheered, as the spirit moved them, until this convention, which Republican newspapers characterized as "one of the best natured political gatherings ever witnessed in the state," actually did degenerate into "a howling mob" and "outrivalled Pandemonium."

The ticket was headed by one of the chief fuglemen of the Railroad party, and before it was completed the convention actually fought, raved and howled like maniacs over the nominations for attorney general and other offices which are supposed to carry dignity with them, but carried anything else in this instance.

Among the things performed by this so-called "good natured Republican convention" was the cold-blooded and ruthless sacrifice they made of two state officials who were before the convention seeking endorsement for their services to their party through a second nomination. Unfortunately for these two gentlemen they had served their party not wisely but too well.

At the dictation of; the corporation masters of their party they had performed an official act which materially reduced the assessment of railroad property in the state thereby saving to the corporations probably $100,000 in taxes. While this act was part of the reward the railroad corporations of the state were to receive for their political services to the republican party, the responsibility fell upon the individual members of the board of railway assessors, and the two members of that board seeking renomination were ruthlessly sacrificed—not because the leaders of the republican party did not approve of their action, but because they hoped by this sacrifice to appease the wrath of an outraged people, and by a pretended virtue to deceive the discontented masses into once more voting the Republican ticket.

On July 6, the Democratic State Convention was held in the same hall and its conduct and action were in marked contrast with those of its immediate predecessor. It was a strictly representative gathering of the Kansas Democracy, and when questions came up on which there was a difference of opinion they were debated with strength, eloquence and manliness by the delegates.

It was held by a very large majority that the vital issue in the campaign was the overthrow of the corrupt and dominant Republican party, and that the only means to this end was the solid union of the opposition forces. By a vote of 390 to 39 the electoral ticket of the Wichita convention was indorsed, and after a protracted debate, the State ticket named by the People's party was likewise indorsed though by a less) a majority, the vote standing 227 for are 76 against a combination that would . are Republican defeat on November 8 and redeem the State from the control of the mercenaries who represented Wall Street and . the great railroad corporations.

It was in this debate that Senator John Martin showed himself to be a very lion on the floor, and that he was still the intrepid leader of the Kansas Democracy, in which for more than a score of years he had been Chairman of the State Central Committee at a time when that party was so small that year after year its annual conventions were held in his own law office in the City of Topeka. The result of his gallant struggle on this ∨

occasion was received with thunders of applause, though a handful of erstwhile Democratic wheel-horses left the hall to organize later the so-called Stalwart Democratic party, and, as assistant Republicans, exert every effort to retain the corporation party in power.

Their pretended convention at the Grand Opera House in Topeka on October 7, was the last of a quartette of State political assemblies that are destined to become memorable in the history of Kansas. The troublous and stormy sea of politics in the Sunflower State never tossed up a stranger bit of wreck and drift than this same convention, made up of railroad attorneys and corporation hirelings who came to the capital city on passes issued by the hundreds, to demonstrate the extent of their vassalage to the brass-colored monopolists. From the stage, former Democratic leaders whose principles had been lost sight of by long service in the pay of corporations, openly avowed their intention of voting the straight Republican ticket from top to bottom, and denounced in unmeasured terms the movement of the combined forces of the opposition to rid Kansas of a tyranny that had impoverished the state and the people, and reduced to serfdom that large class of the rural population whose toil amid privations and dangers of every description had wrested the soil from savage tribes, made Kansas the foremost of the od producing states in the Great Central Basin, and enriched the railroads and the money princes of the east to an extent unheard of in all the history of the Western Continent.

The issues were now made up, and the corporation party was squarely arrayed against the people.

From early autumn to November 8 a vigorous campaign was fought night and day by both political forces.

It was a veritable war of the Titans, a struggle to the death by two powerful combatants. It was a battle for liberty on the one side, and on the other for the perpetuation in power of men who had cast principles to the wind, bartered for gold the glory of the party founded by Lincoln, and who would place on the wrists of the freemen of the Great West the shackles struck from the

black race in the South thirty years ago.

Well might the issue be watched with anxiety from every section of the land, and every toiler in the state enroll himself for the fray. And well might the corporations unlock their treasure vaults and turn loose a flood of gold to check the tide that was setting in with a force that threatened to sweep their paid agents forever from power in the councils of the state.

As it became more and more evident to the Republican party toward the close of the campaign that defeat was inevitable, the leaders began devising iniquitous schemes for robbing the people of the fruits of victory. Where fraud and bribery could not prevail at the polls, the matter would be settled to their liking, either before the State Board of Canvassers, where the whole election machinery was in the hands of as corrupt a gang of Republican partisans as ever existed, or, if that method failed, another—more remote, more dark, more revolutionary —would be resorted to.

The great day dawned at last, the battle waged furiously all along the line, and right triumphed. It was so unmistakably a complete and overwhelming victory for the people that no room was left for either party to doubt. The Republicans were dismayed as the returns began to come in. In fact they were panic stricken and required time to study over the situation. It was probably to accommodate them in this respect that the Kansas City Journal of November 9 came out with something very like a stereotyped copy of the article it published on the morning after the election of 1890, claiming everything in sight for its party, and kept up these claims for the rest of the week.

With singular unity of purpose the Topeka Capital of November 9 claimed the election of the Republican State ticket by "at least 12,000," and that "the electoral ticket will fall less than 3,000 behind." "Kansas Redeemed" was the truthful headline on its telegraph page, but the redemption was not according to the Capital's standard and meaning.

Editorially, the same paper, under the head of "Glorious for Kansas," said:

In the Republican gloom that has struck the party nationally like a total eclipse, one grand redeeming light shines out from Kan-

sas. To paraphrase the lines of Words-
worth, Kansas looms up out of the darkness

Fair as a star when only one
    Is shining in the sky.
It is a great victory. * * * The victory
means everything to Kansas. It means redemption and regeneration. It means notice to the people of the nation that intelligence and integrity rule again in the state.
It means renewed immigration and influx
of capital. It means that apologies for
Kansas need no longer be demanded. It
means that property is safe and that repu-
pudiation is itself repudiated. * * * The
indications point not only to the election of
the state ticket and a good working majority
in the state legislature, but to the defeat of
every Populist congressman. * * *

Here again were wise words spoken, if not
in jest, intended at least to deceive. Kansas
did indeed shine forth as a bright, particular
star, and the language of the Capital's edi-
torial reads like a prophesy, or would if the
word "Populist" was substituted for that of
"Republican." It was "a victory that means
everything to Kansas," redemption, regeneration, and the rule of intelligence, renewed
immigration and influx of capital.

But, a day later, "a change came o'er the
spirit of the Capital's dream," for even that
redoubtable republican sheet admitted
"Kansas in doubt," and reduced the republican majority from 12,000 to 4,500, which,
it said editorially, meant that—

The democracy has enabled calamity to
menace, if not actually to capture, the state.

The republicans of Kansas were advised
to begin the campaign of 1894 that very
day, and subsequent events proved that the
advice was acted upon. The political situation then became "a blot on the record of
the democracy that will never be effaced;"
"a disgraceful liason with calamity," and
all that sort of thing.

It was Sunday morning before the Capital began to explain "Why We Lost," and
by some remarkable process of computing
figures to show that while the railroad party
was undoubtedly snowed under the returns
showed a net gain of 60,000 in the strength
of the republican vote of Kansas.

Meantime the allied forces were rejoicing
in the certainty of a grand victory. Blanks
had been sent out to all sections to be filled
with copies of the returns and forwarded
promptly to headquarters. This request
was very generally complied with, the returns pouring in immediately, and

each gave fresh assurance of the utter rout
of the common enemy and the vindication
of the rights of the people.

THE CONSPIRACY.

THE MASK BOLDLY THROWN ASIDE BY THE RE-
PUBLICANS.—INFAMIES PERPETRATED BY THE
STATE CANVASSING BOARD.—THE ROSENTHAL
CASE.—THE COFFEY COUNTY CASE.—AN OKLA-
HOMA CITIZEN "CERTIFICATED."

Stirring as were the events of the summer
and autumn preceding the overthrow of the
Republican party, they were but the preface
of one volume of Kansas history that will
stand through all time pre-eminent in interest to the student of Kansas politics. In its
defiance of the public will, its knowledge of
the entire support of the railroads and other
corporations in its fell designs, its supreme
conceit and confidence that no combination
of interests could depose it from power, the
dominant party had to a degree concealed
its desperate determination to win at all
hazards and had thus far created anxiety,
but not absolute alarm.

Now the mask was thrown aside and the
suspicion that it would attempt to defeat the
will of the people became a terrible and
alarming certainty.

There was soon no longer room to doubt
that the corporation powers of the state
were conspiring against the voters, and that,
having lost control of the Executive department of the Government, they would reck-
lessly and unblushingly make an attempt to
hold the legislative branch by stealing the
seats of the Populist Representatives-elect,
so far as was necessary in order to secure the
organization of the house, and the ultimate
election of a United State Senator and a
State Printer. Unparalleled frauds had
been committed by unprincipled Republicans at the polls and on the county canvassing boards, but it was left for the State
Canvassing Board to perpetrate the crowning infamy and reveal the atrocious scheme

of the conspirators in all its hideous details.

The State Canvassing Board met in Topeka on November 28 All the members—Governor Humphrey, Treasurer Stover, Auditor Hovey, secretary of State Higgins, State Superintendent Winans and Attorney General Ives—were present. There had already been much "deplomacy" exercised in order to enable this board to carry out the will of its masters. The returns had been opened and examined. Where corrupt county canvassing boards had not counted out populist representatives .or overlooked clerical errors (?) that would elect Republican members, preparations had been made to complete the work in this board. Where irregularities occurred that would work injuriously to the Populist cause, the returns were held back until too late for correcti jn, but where mistakes appeared that would be disastrous to Republican interests pains were taken to have them rectified without delay.

The first interesting development before the State Board of Canvassers was the discovery of an irregularity in the returns from Sedgwick and Wilson Counties on the People's party candidates for Presidential Electors. In the case of E. B. Cabbell, one of these Electoral candidates, the returns were made to read E. B. Campbell, instead of E. B. Cabbell. It was apparent that this was a clerical error but the vote was thrown out and the county clerks telegraphed to learn whether it was really a clerical error, or whether the ballots were printed that way. As there were over 6,000 ballots of that sort it was enough to defeat Cabbell, which would give the Republicans one out of ten of the Presidential Electors, and this would leave matters in shape to aid the national pa ty to that extent in the Electoral College if the vote should be very close.

On the following day the board held that the manifest error could not be corrected and o motion of Col. Bill Higgins resolved that it "had no legal authority to make any changes of the returns as certified by the various County Clerks, nor has said board any authority to call for or demand any amendatory or supplementary returns."

"This," remarked the Capital next morning, "knocks out Mr. Cabbell (colored), one

of the People's party presidential electors. But it did not, for the board, after an immense amount of trouble, was compelled to reconvene, correct the error and declare;Mr. Cabbell elected.

But with characteristic inconsistency, the board refused to correct a somewhat similar error, but one not less apparent, in the Haskell county case. Here the county clerk made a transposition of the figures, and instead of giving Joe Rosenthal, straight democratic candidate for representative, 156 votes, and A. W. Stubbs, the Republican candidate, 123, reversed the figures. Stubbs was necessary to the Republicans [to] make up their majority in the House, and on these returns, despite an absolute knowledge that they were wrong, the Board issued a certificate to Mr. Stubbs.

Yet high-handed and arbitrary as were the proceedings of the Board in the latter case, they were exceeded in brazen effrontry by its action on the Coffey county case, where the returns, grossly irregular, showed on their face a tie between Rice, the Populist candidate, and Ballinger, his Republican opponent. The decision in this instance was postponed until the last da, 's session, when everything else had been completed. General Ives had objected to casting lots to determine who should be given the certificate, as being unconstitutional, but he was overruled. In such cases, where the statute requires a casting of lots by the State canvassers, it must be done in the presence of both the interested parties, but even that formality was dispensed with. Without notice to Ballinger, the Board went into secret session and remained with closed doors for an hour and a half During this time the drawing is alleged to have taken place, the slips being drawn from a hat by Bill Higgins. The decisive slip was reached by him at the ninth drawing, and, it is unnecessary to add, it read "Republican." And the Republican candidate for Representative from Coffey county was declared elected.

The members of the board then unlocked the door and came out with their overcoats on, announced in an off hand way that they had decided in favor of Ballinger, and stated as they left the capital that the Board had adjourned *sine die.*

By unseating Rosenthal and Rice, the Republicans had been secured a majority of two in the house and this fact, together with the Star Chamber method of settling the Coffey county tie, confirmed the suspicion that the conspiracy was dangerously deep, and the conspirators desperately determined to succeed in their nefarious plot to reverse the decision of the people at the polls.

One of the most glaring frauds perpetrated by the Republicans in their conspiracy to capture the legislature was in the election of M. B. Chrisman, a citizen of Oklahoma, as representative from Chautauqua county. His opponent was A. M. Ross. Higgins "certificated" him, notwithstanding the facts concerning his citizenship of an adjacent commonwealth were well known.

M. B. Chrisman had, as early as April 2⁷, 1892, declared under oath his good faith and intention *to become a permanent resident and citizen of Oklahoma Territory*, and to cultivate and personally occupy and make his home upon the land which he then laid claim to in that territory. Under the sworn declaration which he then made his actual settlement upon the land might be postponed until six months later: but on the 18th day of July, 1892, there being no prior adverse right to the land, Chrisman, *under oath, declared that such permanent residence and citizenship of Oklahoma*, and such occupation of said land should commence at that date.

This was the condition at the time of the election, November 8, 1892, and there is a note indorsed on the back of his application indicating that he had obtained a leave of absence on the 2d day of November, 1892. But there is no uncertainty as to the conditions on December 10, 1892. On that day he was before an officer of Kingfisher county, in the territory of Oklahoma, where he made an affidavit of facts, which were corroborated by Isaac Chrisman and M. D. Chrisman, whose address was Dover, Kingfisher county, Oklahoma territory.

In this affidavit Chrisman swears that his present postoffice address *will be* Wauneta, Chautauqua county, Kansas; that he was the identical person who, on the 18th day of July, 1892, made the homestead entry on the land mentioned; that he had built on said land a one and one-half story frame dwelling house, had dug a well and broken out ten acres of the land; that his improvements thereon aggregated $200 in value; *that he had established his personal residence on said land, and resided there continually since December 3, 1892;* and he wanted leave of absence to gather his corn crops in the field, and to give his personal attention to other matters at his "old home in Kansas," desiring to return with his family and *resume his residence* on the land after his temporary absence.

Section 4, Article 2, of the Constitution of Kansas, declares: "No person shall be a member of the Legislature who is not, at the time of his election, a qualified voter of and a resident in the county or district for which he is elected." In view of this provision, there can be no doubt that it is the plain intendment of the Constitution that Senators and Representatives are chosen for the purpose of representing a particular district in which he resides, and for which he was chosen, and that whenever he removes from such Senatorial or Representative district he can no longer legally represent the people of such district. It necessarily follows that Mr. Chrisman, whether he was a legal resident of the Fifty-first Representative District on the 8th of November, 1892, or not, had acquired a *bona fide* residence in the Territory of Oklahoma, according to his affidavit, and that whatever right he had acquired, if any, under his supposed election on the 8th of November last, was lost to him, and that he could not legally hold a seat as a Representative in the Kansas House of Representatives.

Yet in the face of these facts Higgins had the audacity, in order to carry out the orders of his masters, the corporation managers, to deliver to him his certificate of election, and it may be inferred that he would have done the same thing a dozen times over had the circumstances demanded it.

THE MANDAMUS CASES.

WHAT QUESTIONS WERE INVOLVED AND WHAT
DECIDED—THE POSSIBLE EFFECT OF THE
DECISIONS UPON POLITICAL QUESTIONS THAT
MAY ARISE HEREAFTER.

The returning board was not, however, the
only authoritative source to which the Republicans felt they might look for aid and
comfort in carrying out their conspiracy
against the people of Kansas. The opposition, on the other hand, did not anticipate a
denial of justice at the hands of the highest legal tribunal in the state.

Much has been said about the mandamus
cases in the Supreme Court before the Legislature convened. There were four such
cases, and what questions were involved
and what questions were decided, are not
clearly understood by the people; much less
is it generally understood what effect the
decisions made in those cases had upon the
subsequent organization or political complexion of the Legislature, or may have upon
questions which are likely to arise hereafter.
Let us briefly state what these four cases
were, and in the order in which they were
commenced and decided in the Supreme
court.

In Haskell County Joseph Rosenthal received 156 votes, and A. W. Stubbs 123 votes
for Representative. The county commissioners as a board of canvassers ascertained
and declared that result, and declared that
Joseph Rosenthal was elected. The county
clerk, either through accident or design,
transposed the figures, and certified to the
Secretary of State that Rosenthal's vote was
123 and Stubbs's vote 156. This mistake
was undoubtedly known to everybody
long before the canvass was made by the
State Board of Canvassers, and there is
much reason to believe that the returns
upon which the state canvass was based had
been altered or substituted for the returns
first made by the county clerk. Be that as
it may, the public press of the state had
continuously published the fact that Mr.
Rosenthal had been elected Representative
from Haskell County. When the official
canvass was made and published, stating
that Mr. Stubbs was elected, the whole state
was amazed. Rosenthal brought mandamus in the Supreme Court to compel the
State Board of Canvassers to recanvass the
vote, and to award the certificate of election
to him. It was generally understood, not
only among newspaper men, but among
lawyers as well, that Rosenthal's case was
so clear that the court would decide
in his favor. It was admitted on
all hands, and admitted as a fact at
the trial in the Supreme Court, and admitted by the Judges of the Court themselves,
that Rosenthal had been elected, and yet by
reason of the state canvass the certificate of
election had been awarded to Stubbs. The
Court decided against Rosenthal. Not only
this, but it decided against law, and against
equity, and against justice. It based its decision upon the single point, that the State
Board of Canvassers "had acted upon the
question, and had adjourned without day"
—that its functions had been fully performed, and that as a body it was dead. Outrageous as this decision was, the effect of it
was, and will be, if adhered to, that whenever the State Board of Canvassers or any
other Board of Canvassers shall have acted
upon any question properly before them,
and shall have "adjourned without day," the
action of such Board is final to that degree
and extent that errors committed, either
through ignorance, carelessness or villainy,
cannot be corrected by the Courts. And that
is all there was in the Rosenthal case.

In Coffey County, O. M. Rice and T. C.
Ballinger were opposing candidates for
member of the House of Representatives.
The returns made to the County Clerk by
the Judges of Election gave Ballinger 1,826
votes, and gave Rice 1,827 votes. Two of
the County Commissioners, constituting a
majority of the Board of Canvassers, and
against the protest of the third member,
when making the county canvass, deliberately altered the returns from Avon Township, which had given and returned ninety-
six votes for Rice, so as to make the returns
read ninety-five votes for Rice, and then
upon this forgery and fraud, with the re-

turns from the other precincts, the County Canvassers declared that Ballinger had received 1,826 votes, and that Rice had received 1,826 votes, making a tie between them. The County Clerk certified to the Secretary of State the vote as canvassed by the Commissioners of his County, and the State Board declared a tie to exist, and then proceeded "to cast lots," as they said, and of course Ballinger was successful, and received the certificate of election. It was a common remark at the time that the "casting of lots" was a mere farce. Mr. Higgins states in his official report that sixteen blank strips of paper, together with two other strips on one of which was written "Populist" and the other "Republican," were put in the hat, and that the drawing took place from that hat until the slip with the word "Republican" upon it was drawn; and that meant the election of Ballinger. The people generally believed, and still believe, that of the eighteen slips that were put into the hat, eight or ten of them had "Republican" written upon them, and that all the others were blank, thus making Mr. Ballinger's election by the Higgins outfit certain. But when Mr. Rice discovered the fraud which had been committed by the commissioners of Coffey county, he commenced mandamus proceedings in the supreme court to compel the County Commissioners as canvassers to meet and canvass the votes for Representative as returned by the judges of election. Upon the hearing of this case the County Clerk and County Commissoners were required to attend and produce their records, and did so. The fraud and forgery respecting the vote of Avon township, as stated above, was then made apparent by the records themselves; but the supreme court denied the writ of mandamus, upon the theory, that a paper unknown to the law, called a tally-list, had been returned by the judges of election, which tally-list showed that Rice had received only 1,826 votes, and this decision was fortified by following the rule adopted in the Rosenthal case, namely, "the Board of Canvassers having adjourned without day," the Court was powerless to compel it to reconvene and correct the error, even if there was one. And that is all there was of the Coffey county case. The decision of the Court upon both points was contrary to law,

and was alike inequitable and unjust.

The Jackson County case was this: The Legislature of 1891 assigned two Representatives to Jackson County, but in making the apportionment the city of Holton was omitted from both districts. Under the law there was no more reason for believing that the city of Holton was in one district, than there was for believing that it was in the other district. In the Northern district Ed. Shellabarger and Nick Kline were opposing candidates for Representative. The election was duly held and returns were duly made to the County Clerk from every precinct in the district as the district had been defined by law, and such returns gave Shellabarger 629 votes, and Kline 554 votes. The returning officers for the city of Holton returned votes as having been cast in that city, some for Shellabarger, but a larger number for Kline, which votes, added to those cast in the district, gave a majority for Kline. The County Commissioners canvassed the whole vote, including that returned from the city of Holton, and the County Clerk, instead of certifying to the Secretary of State the vote as cast by Townships or Precincts, simply certified the total vote cast as ascertained and declared by the County Commissioners. Upon the returns so certified by the County Clerk the State board would, of course, issue the certificate of election to Kline. Shellabarger, believing that it was the Legislature that created districts and made laws, and not boards of county commissioners or county canvassers, commenced mandamus proceedings in the Supreme Court to compel the Commissioners of Jackson County and the County Clerk to recanvass the vote and to certify the facts as above stated. The Supreme Court refused to grant the writ of mandamus, holding, without any legal evidence to support the proposition, that the Legislature had intended to make Holton a part of the Northern district, and saying that the question as to whether Shellabarger or Kline should be admitted to a seat was one for the House of Representatives itself and not for the courts, concluded to exercise its "discretion," and refused the mandamus, which, of course, allowed the certificate issued by the Higgins outfit to stand. This decision was wrong in this, that it is the duty of the County Canvassers to canvass the vote from every precinct within the township, district or county created by law, for which township, district or county they constitute a Board of Canvassers. The County Canvassers have no more right to enlarge a Representative district than they have to enlarge their county and canvass votes outside their county. The decision of the Supreme Court was simply to let the outrage committed by the Commissioners of Jackson county stand uncorrected by judicial decision. And that is all there is of the Jackson County case.

The Republic County case was this: The apportionment act of 1886 divided Republic county into two representative districts, numbering them respectively as districts seventy-three and seventy-four. The apportionment act of 1891 made Republic County a single district, and numbered it sixty-one. At the election of 1892 J. M. Foster and J. W. Wilds were opposing candidates for Representative. In some of the townships votes were cast and returned for each candidate as having been cast in district numbered "73," and the county canvass so stated. The county clerk certified the canvass to the Secretary of State as made by the county board. The Higgins outfit added these together, and by so doing, gave the certificate of election to Foster, whereas, had they simply acted upon the votes returned as having been cast in "district 61," Wilds would have been entitled to the certificate. Wilds, not claiming that he had been elected by a majority of the votes cast in his county, nevertheless claimed that the error which was committed by placing the wrong district on the ballots was one which the State Board of Canvassers could not correct, but which the House of Representatives alone could determine; and so he commenced mandamus against the State Board of Canvassers to compel them to canvass the votes as returned to them by the County Clerk of Republic county, and award him the certificate of election. The Supreme Court held, and perhaps correctly in this case, that the designation of a district on a ballot was wholly unnecessary, and that the vote cast in the whole county should have been canvassed as an entirety, and the result declared accordingly, and so refused the writ of mandamus asked for by Wilds. This case

decided nothing except as already stated, that it is unnecessary to designate the district on the ticket or ballot

These are the four cases which were decided it the Supreme Court before the Legislature met. They had not and could not have any effect whatever upon the organization of the House of Representatives, or upon determining the status of any member, or of any party, except that in the Haskell and Coffey county cases, the court refused to exercise the powers it possessed to correct a wrong which had been committed in the one case by the County Clerk, and in the other by the County Commissioners.

INAUGURAL DAY.

A NOTABLE GATHERING AT REPRESENTATIVE HALL—THE END OF REPUBLICAN DOMINATION—"A GOVERNMENT OF THE PEOPLE, BY THE PEOPLE AND FOR THE PEOPLE."—SEEDS OF DISCORD SOWN.

On Monday, January 10, the entire machinery of state was, for the first time in the history of Kansas, surrendered by the Republican party, whose representatives in the various departments of the capitol building reluctantly yielded the reins of government to the People's party. During the thirty years in which they had retained control there was never such a monster demonstration at the inauguration of a new Governor and a new administration as on this occasion, nor were the ceremonies ever before so imposing and significant.

Chairman Breidenthal's invitation to the farmers to come to Topeka and see the people's Governor inaugurated had been received with genuine approval, and was very generally accepted. Visitors from the agricultural districts of the State, from the Blue to the Arkansas river valley, and from the Missouri to the foot-hills of the Rockies, came pouring in by hundreds and by thousands, filled with enthusiasm over their grand victory and anticipations of the glorious results to follow. There was probably never before such a gathering assembled in this commonwealth as that which at noon, on January 10, filled Representative hall to watch the inauguration of Governor L. D. Lewelling. Each individual in the vast throng, whose sympathies were with the movement that had relegated Republican rule to the rear, felt, as one of the speakers expressed it, that the great common people were at last to see inaugurated an adminis- tration of their own, and that they would live to see many a repetition of this scene in years to come. They felt that it was "appropriate that in this great State of Kansas, where the first battle was fought for the freedom of the black slave, the battle should be begun that is to free the white slave." They who had en- dured oppression, persecution, and misrep- resentation, and who had borne the brunt of the battle, for once appeared as victors in a triumphed march whose glory was never equalled in the palmiest days of Rome.

There were hundreds of Republicans pres- ent, too, and a vast number of ladies of every political party, while the entire roster of retiring state officials attended with the object of appearing to "take their medi- cine" serenely. Then there were the lead- ers of the now dominant party, whose ban- ners had led the Populist hosts to victory, and whose bosoms doubtless swelled with pride at this magnificent ovation from their loyal and devoted followers. Among those who were the object of especial attention were John Willits, Judge Rightmire, Con- gressman Simpson, Levi Dumbauld, Dr. McLallin, S. S. King, S M. Scott, Dick Chase, S. H. Snider, J. R. Detwiler, Charles Moody, Colonel F. J. Close, Messrs. House- holder and Yount, with a score of others equally celebrated for gallant work for the people's cause. Mrs. Mary E. Lease was the observed of all observers and there was also present a distinguished visitor in the person of Hon. A. J. Streeter, of Illinois, who in 1888 was the candidate of the Union Labor party for vice-president.

Representative hall was superbly decor- ated and never looked so beautiful as on this occasion. The brightest evergreens en- circled with many a fold the electric lamps of the great chandelier suspended from the central ceiling, almost concealing that mag- nificent ornament from view. From this emerald mid-air bower—a miniature hang- ing garden of Babylon—cables of like ma- terial extended to the corners of the hall, the strands made firmer by knots of red rib- bon. More evergreens, fluttering flags and rich floral ornaments adorned the walls, while the speaker's stand was fairly buried beneath the lavish display of tropical plants and the whole was crowned by a great basket of choicest roses, resting on the desk of the presiding officer.

Above the main entrance to the spacious room was the picture of John Brown, the hero of Osawatomie and of Harper's Ferry; on either side of the speaker's desk, the familiar likenesses of Washington and Lin- coln; on the north and south walls, life size portraits of the ex-governors of Kansas, and, most conspicious of all, the state's great flag, its graceful folds lashed to the gallery pillars with wreaths of evergreen and roses.

A few moments before 11 o'clock, the ladies of the Shawnee County Alliance ap- peared on the platform and unfolded to the view of the audience a gleaming banner of silk, trimmed with gold bullion and bear- ing, in letters of gold, the familiar motto of the Farmers' Alliance:

A GOVERNMENT

Of the People, By the People

And For the People,

Shall Not Perish.

A. LINCOLN.

At this sight a great shout went up, and the wave of enthusiasm rose still higher when there was displayed in the most prom- inent part of the hall, a life-size portrait of Governor Lewelling, done by a Topeka artist.

Oh, it was a glorious day for those loyal people who had stood up for Kansas in her hour of peril, and at a time when the ruling power had reduced them to the condition almost of serfs, while yet retaining as sov- ereign citizens of the Republic, a full knowl- edge of the grievous wrongs to which they had been subjected.

The hands of the big clock in Representative Hall had barely met at the meridian hour, when Governor Lewelling, accompanied by Mrs. Lewelling, and their daughters, Jessie and Pauline, entered the room, closely followed by the new State officials, and these in turn by Governor Humphrey and the retiring officials of the outgoing administration.

Hon. John W. Breidenthal, chairman of the People's Party State Central Committee, called the assembly to order and said:

We have assembled here to witness the inaugural ceremonies of the first People's party administration on earth. That the new party will have the good will of the people of Kansas is made evident by the magnificent audience which greets us here to-day.

He then introduced the Rev. W. G. Todd, who in a brief prayer implored the Almighty that the men who had been given control of the affairs of state might prove to be men who could stand for the right and the truth, whatever temptations should confront them.

Governor L. U. Humphrey was then introduced by Chairman Breidenthal, and, accompanied by his successor, advanced to the platform amid the heartiest applause. His farewell address gracefully recognized the fitness of his "worthy successor" to meet the high responsibilities of the office, which he said he surrendered with pleasure and satisfaction. In conclusion, Governor Humphrey said: "I have now the pleasure and satisfaction of introducing to you my honored and worthy successor, Governor Lewelling."

This was the signal for an outburst of applause that made the walls fairly tremble, and as Governor Lewelling advanced to the front of the platform the cheering assumed an increased vigor, while many of the more enthusiastic partisans present threw their hats in the air and in other ways evinced their feelings of joy.

The Governor's inaugural address was delivered with an earnestness, ease, grace and eloquence that won the cordial approval of even his bitterest opponents, and at its conclusion his adherents felt that their standard bearer was in every way worthy of their trust and had vindicated the high cause for which they had striven so long, so earnestly and so successfully.

At the conclusion of his address the oath of office was administered to Governor Lewelling by Chief Justice Horton, and the formal announcement was made that he was now the chief executive of Kansas. The great seal of state was handed over to Governor Lewelling by his predecessor, and the several officers of the new administration were successively introduced by the retiring incumbents and took their official oaths, each placing his right hand upon the Bible, and afterwards imprinting a kiss upon the Book.

The inaugural exercises occupied exactly an hour, within which brief time a change was made that is destined to work favorably, for all time to come, to the welfare of the people of a commonwealth which in breadth of territory, natural resources and population surpasses the majority of the kingdoms, principalities and grand duchies of the Old World, and which to-day is known by name more widely in foreign lands than even the Great Republic of which it is but one of the forty-four sovereign states.

The details of this day's proceedings have been dwelt upon at this length because it is felt that never in the history of Kansas was there an occurrence of so much significance to the people, not only of Kansas but of the whole American Union. It was the first signal triumph over plutocracy, the knell of corporation rule, the ushering in of a new era. Once more could it be truthfully said, "The Lord has turned again the captivity of Zion." Those who were present on this occasion will hand down to their children and their children's children, a legend that will be cherished as sacredly and redound as greatly to the credit of the chief actors in the bloodless revolution by which Kansas was redeemed, as fell to the lot of the descendants of the Pilgrim Fathers, the signers of the Declaration of Independence, or the heroes of 1776, who freed this nation from foreign rule.

On the evening of Inaugural Day there was another notable gathering at Representative hall, when the auditorium and galleries were packed with loyal adherents of the new dominant party and patriotic speeches were made by orators who had during the campaign made their influence felt throughout the State. Thus closed a day that will be memorable so long as history shall' chronicle events vitally affecting the welfare of the people, and yet, while there was not a single incident suggesting aught but peace and good will throughout the entire programme, the organ of the corporations next morning announced "A Collision Likely," and' sowed the seeds of discord whose rank growth during the ensuing week was destined to place Kansas before the world in the light of a community in which anarchy reigned supreme and law was more lightly esteemed than the thistle down that floats hither and thither at the mercy of the south wind in the summer season.

THE OVERT ACT.

THE ORGANIZATION OF THE HOUSE OF REPRE-
SENTATIVES—REVOLUTIONARY CONDUCT OF
THE REPUBLICANS—LAW AND PRECEDENT
DEFIED—THE POSITION OF THE PEOPLE'S
PARTY—BIRTH OF THE DUAL HOUSE.

High noon of January 10 was the hour set for convening the Lower House of the Kansas Legislature, which, because of the remarkable condition of affairs already outlined and of the determination of the Republican conspirators to capture the organization, was destined to have the most turbulent career of any similar body ever assembled in the state.

For weeks the agents of the corporation party had spread broadcast at home and heralded abroad through the medium of special correspondents, the report that serious trouble, if not an actual collision between armed factions, would attend the organization of the House of Representatives. Open threats were made and boastful and exaggerated claims indulged in, which had the effect of awakening unprecedented interest in the preliminary proceedings. It was apparent that every means would be resorted to by the Republicans to secure control of this body and in order to cover their own insidious designs they gave

it out that their opponents were massing a; armed force at the capital to overawe the authorities and seize by force of arms the right and power with which they had bee entrusted by the vote of the people at tl November election. It had undoubtedl; been agreed beforehand by the Republicans, that, if necessary, force should be resorted to and these rumors were designed to give a color of excuse for striking another blow at the liberty of the people and inaugurating civil war in Kansas.

The elaborate decorations of the hall which still remained as on Inauguration Day—the evergreens and the flowers, the flags and the banners, the portraits of Washington, of Lincoln, and of "Osawatomie Brown," as well as the pioneer Governors of the Sunflower State—seemed a hollow mockery in view of the menacing aspect of the situation.

The floor of the House was reserved for the members and officers, while the galleries, open to the public, were filled to their utmost capacity, and many who held tickets were unable to obtain admission by reason of the dense throng, which included many ladies interested in the proceedings from one cause or another. Their presence and that of so large a number of distinguished Kansans, reminded one insensibly of the magnificent description given by Macauley of the trial of Warren Hastings. For "the fair-haired daughters of the House of Brunswick" were substituted the no less fair daughters of the Sunflower State, while the judiciary and state-craft were equally well represented.

Among the first to appear on the floor were Messrs. Rosenthal and Stubbs, the former of whom was, especially, an object of attention to those interested in the outcome.

It was precisely 1:30 o'clock when Secretary of State Osborn appeared with the duly-certified roll of Representatives elect, as shown by the records in his office, and rapped the House to order. He explained that, in accordance with the precedents long ago established in Kansas and other commonwealths of the Union, it was the unanimous desire of the Representatives of the People's party that he should act as presiding officer, pending the temporary organization of the House, and made, in substance, the following statement:

Gentlemen of Kansas, the law requires me to lay before the Senate and House of Representatives a list of its members as shown by the returns in my office. It has been customary, as I understand, in the past, for the secretary of state to act as presiding officer prior to effecting temporary organization, but as I find no law conferring that authority upon me, I do not care to usurp or assume it unless by unanimous consent.

Scarcely had Secretary Osborn completed the statement of his position in the premises, when George L. Douglass, of Wichita, the caucus nominee of the Republicans for Speaker, and in a measure regarded as the leader of that faction on the floor of the new House at that moment ushered into existence, arose and, addressing the Secretary, plunged without delay into the vital question involved in the organization. He assumed boldly that it was not the prerogative of the Secretary of State to continue to act as presiding officer after having laid before the House the roll of members as reported to his office, unless called upon by a majority of the House to do so.

Mr. J. M. Dunsmore, of Neosho, representing the Populist side, secured recognition and addressing the Secretary of State, insisted that, in accordance with precedents long established, the Secretary should act as the Chairman, pending the temporary organization. He argued that the recognition of Secretary Osborn by Mr. Douglass had already made him the de facto Chairman of the body, and took the ground that objections to certain names on the roll of members should be heard and passed upon before the roll was regularly submitted.

Mr. Douglass, in reply, urged that there was no warrant or authority for the Secretary of State acting as temporary chairman of the body, and insisted upon his objections being held good, and that the Secretary lay the roll before the House before reading it.

Mr. Dunsmore, in answer to this, said that, in accordance with recognized rules and precedents, the Populists believed it to be their right to challenge the name of any person appearing upon the roll whom they had reason to believe was either not duly elected to a seat in this House, or who for any reason was disqualified to occupy the same. He further submitted the following proposition:

"We," meaning the Representatives of the People's party, "are willing that a temporary organization be effected by the vote of members elected whose seats are not disputed, or by the votes of all persons claiming seats in this body in good faith."

This proposition was rejected by Mr. Douglass, representing the Republicans, and thereupon the Secretary of State said:

"I repeat again that the law requires me to lay before each house a list of its members. I have just performed this duty in the Senate, where I found a presiding officer to whom I delivered the list. Whenever this House has a presiding officer to whom I can deliver the list, and I am apprised of that fact I shall appear before you again, and deliver the official list to such officer."

Secretary Osborn thereupon retired from the hall and left the assembled claimants for seats in the House of Representatives without any person to whom they could address themselves for the purpose of making motions or otherwise providing for a temporary organization.

It was at this juncture that Hon. R. H. Semple, of Franklin, one of the duly elected and qualified Representatives, whose seat was not in dispute, appeared at the Speaker's desk and taking up the official gavel assumed the authority of calling the House to order. This, it is claimed, he had a right to do upon that fundamental and universally recognized rule of the common law that he who is first in time is first in right, Mr. Semple's only object being to call the House to order and preside until a temporary Chairman was elected.

This eminently proper course was, however, by no means in accord with the wishes of the Republican leaders nor conducive to the success of the conspiracy. As is now apparent, they had intended from the outset to subvert the will of the people of Kansas, in obedience to the desire and dictation of their corporation masters, and the time had arrived for the commission of the overt act by the prevention of a fair and impartial investigation into the rights by which the seats were claimed in this House. To this end they had provided themselves with a certified copy of the report of the returning

board, which one of them had in his possession in anticipation of that which next occurred and which they had previously
planned.

Immediately after the assumption by Mr.
Semple of the position of temporary presiding officer, George L. Douglass sprang to
his feet and nominated Mr. Cubbison, of
Kansas City, Kan., for temporary chairman.
The Republican representatives and Republican claimants voted for Mr. Cubbison
unanimously and that moment the dual
House of Representatives was born, and the
complications, perplexities, wrongs and injustice that were to be heaped upon the opposition for weeks to come were inaugurated.

Each of the presiding office s began rap-
ping for order and in the twinkling of an
eye the body was precipitated into a perfect
bedlam of confusion. Each speaker shouted
at the top of his voice in the vain effort to
drown the voices of competing speakers and
render their motions unintelligible. A veritable pandemonium ensued, in which everybody seemed to be talking without anybody
being heard. There was imminent danger
of a resort to personal violence, which was
averted only by the coolness and prudence
of the Representatives of the People's
party. In the midst of the confusion Mr.
Cubbison entertained a motion from the
Republican side of the House that a roll
of members be read, and the duplicate list
of the returning board was produced and
its reading was proceeded with.

Both sides of the House, in which a complete division had by this time taken place,
now began the work of perfecting a permanent organization.

Chairman Semple was succeeded by Mr.
Ryan, of Crawford, who had been chosen
temporary Speaker, who, in turn, gave way
to Mr. J. M. Dunsmore, elected permanent
Speaker of the House, Mr. Semple being
elected Speaker pro tem.

George L. Douglass, the regular caucus
nominee of the Republicans, was chosen
permanent Speaker of the rival House.

Each of the contending factions appointed
a committee to wait upon the Governor and
notify him that the House was duly organized and ready for business, and pending the recognition of the legal House by
the executive, the members settled down for
a struggle that was to be as protracted as it
was unprecedented in the exciting events attending it.

In arrogating to themselves the right to
organize the House, and pretending so to
organize it by themselves, the Republicans
were guilty of gross usurpation and of the
violation of every law and precedent. They
left to the Representatives of the People's
party no alternative but to either unjustly
surrender their rights, or t) firmly assert by
legal and proper means that they had duly
elected a majority of the members of this
House, the undisputed evidence of which is
to be found upon their journal.

In an authorized statement of the proceedings and rights claimed by the House of
which J. M. Dunsmore was Speaker, which
statement was adopted in the form of a resolution, and appears upon the House Journal (pages 140 to 146) the following precedent is quoted:

It must be remembered that this is not the
first occasion that like conditions confronted
a legislative body: we are, therefore, not
without precedent in this case. At the organization of the twenty-sixth congress, the
seats of five members from New Jersey were
contested; they held the certificates. The
contestants claimed to have been elected.
The clerk, having called the roll until the
names of these members were reached, refused to proceed further until the
House should instruct him which
set of names should be called
as the New Jersey delegation. If the
certified members should be set side, the administration party would have a majority,
and could organize the house; otherwise the
opposition could elect the speaker. Motion
after motion was made, but the clerk refused
to put any motion, because he could not decide who were members entitled to
vote. There was a dead-lock for
several days, during which occured
a memorable debate, participated in by some
of the ablest men then known to the country.
Finally the unorganized house, embracing
both New Jersey delegations, organized as a
meeting by choosing John Q. Adams as
chairman; but a motion having been made,
and the chair having appointed tellers, one
of them inquired which set of members from
New Jersey he should count, and
the chair having stated that the
certificated members should be counted,
the struggle began again, and an appeal
from the the chair's ruling having been demanded, the chair declined to entertain the
appeal, inquiring in his turn who should
vote on the appeal. At last it was decided
by a majority of undisputed members that

neither set of members from New Jersey should be permitted to vote for the time being. (See Eighth Congressional Globe.)

It will be seen that the same identical proposition was submitted by Mr. Dunsmore for the People's party, and rejected by Mr. Douglass for the Republican party.

The thorough investigation made after the organization of the House presided over by Mr. Dunsmore, and the appointment of the Committee on Elections, demonstrated beyond question the fact that the People's party did elect the constitutional majority of the House of Representatives, the character of the testimony in support of this assertion being shown by an examination of the journal records of the House.

RELATIVE STRENGTH OF PARTIES.

WHAT THE FACE OE THE RETURNS SHOWED— TWENTY-FIVE CONTESTS INSTITUTED—THE CLAIMS OF THE PEOPLE'S PARTY GREATLY OUTWEIGH THOSE OF THE CORPORATION CONSPIRATORS.

While both Houses are "sleeping on their arms" at the close of the first day's riotous session, it may be well to glance briefly at the respective strength of the contending parties and some of the claims advanced by each.

While the face of the returns showed the election of sixty-five Republicans, fifty-eight Populists and two Democrats, these figures do not denote the precise status of the rival Houses.

The revolutionary body presided over by George L. Douglass consisted of sixty-three Republicans, with whom Wilson, of Meade, elected on an Independent ticket, acted, making a total of sixty-four certificated members.

The legal House of Representatives, presided over by J. M. Dunsmore, included fifty-eight certificated members.

Notwithstanding the decision of the Supreme Court, by which Mr. Rosenthal was deprived of his certificate, the announcement by his opponent, Mr. A. W. Stubbs,

that he would refuse to attempt to take his seat under any circumstances, left Mr. Rosenthal a clear field, and he, together with Messrs. Meagher and Chambers, the other two Democratic Representatives, decided to stay out of all caucuses and act with neither faction for the time being.

On the part of the People's party eighteen contests had been instituted, and on the part of the Republicans seven, and the position of the former was that there were twenty-five members contesting seats whose names should not be called. The facts in four of the contests instituted by the Populists have been outlined in the decisions of the Supreme Court to which they had been taken earlier, and that of a fifth in the case of the Republican resident of Oklahoma already referred to in detail. Six claimants to seats in the House were, at the time of the election, holding positions as postmasters, of whom four were Republicans. As the constitution expressly declares that "No member of Congress or officer of the United States shall be eligible to a seat in the legislature," the Representatives of the People's party claimed that the candidates receiving the next highest number of votes were entitled to the seats aspired to by the ineligible candidates; that due notice of their disqualification had been given their constituents, so that the customary rule of no election in such cases did not apply, and on other equally strong grounds.

As to the remaining contests, they were based upon the grounds of bribery, illegal voting and gross irregularities upon the part of the returning boards by whom the votes in the several districts were canvassed.

On the whole it will be apparent even to the casual reader, who is unfamiliar with the infamous record of the Republicans of Kansas during the exciting events attending the election and the organization of the lower House, that the claims of the People's party greatly outweighed those of the Republicans, and that had an investigation resulted in a favorable decision in a minority of the cases cited the Populists would have had a fair working majority in the House.

Because of the arrogant and unwarranted usurpation of power by the Republicans, ten of the Populist contestants, whose election was established beyond the peradventure of a doubt, were granted like privileges on the floor of the House presided over by J. M. Dunsmore, to those accorded claimants whose seats were in dispute on the floor of the House of which George L. Douglass was Speaker, thus making a total of sixty-eight Populists answering to roll call on that side of the House on the second day of the legislative term. These ten members were:

J. W. Howard, of Doniphan County.
O. M. Rice, of Coffey County.
D. M. Howard, of Shawnee County.
Ed Shellabarger, of Jackson County.
V. Gleason, of Greenwood County.
W. H. White, of Morris County.
H. Helstrom, of McPherson County.
I. N. Goodvin, of Ness County.
F. B. Brown, of Grant County.
John Morrison, of Gray County.

Under the existing condition of affairs at the time of roll call in the rival Houses on Wednesday, January 11, their relative strength was: Populists, sixty-eight! Republicans, sixty-four, including Wilson, Independent; not participating, three, being Messrs. Meagher, Chambers and Rosenthal, Democrats.

THE SENATE ORGANIZATION.

NO SERIOUS COMPLICATIONS ARISE IN THAT BODY—A GOOD WORKING MAJORITY FOR THE PEOPLE'S PARTY—FIVE REPUBLICAN SEATS CONTESTED.

Here it becomes necessary to go back a little and merely allude, for the sake of the uninformed reader, who was not at the time following the course of events, to the fact that the organization of the Senate was effected without any complications of importance interrupting the proceedings or marring the dignity of that august body.

At 12:10 p. m. on Tuesday, January 10, the Senate was called to order by Lieutenant Governor Percy L. Daniels, and the oath of office was administered to all the members except Senator Price, who was absent, by Associate Justice Allen, of the Supreme Court.

Senator L. P. King was elected President

pro tem., and the full roster of officers was chosen before adjournment.

The personnel of the Senate was as follows: People's party, 22; Republican, 15 Democrats, 3.

Contests were instituted in the case of five Republican Senators, viz: Scott, of Allen Carpenter, of Neosho; Danner, of Harvey Thacher, of Douglas, and Metcalf, of Anderson, but with these our narrative has little or nothing to do, as the political complexion of the Senate remained unchanged throughout the session, and the field to which the great struggle was confined was limited to the House of Representatives.

EXECUTIVE RECOGNITION.

GOVERNOR LEWELLING COMMUNICATES WITH THE SPEAKER OF THE POPULIST HOUSE—OUTSIDE INFLUENCE BROUGHT TO BEAR TO WIDEN THE BREACH BETWEEN THE TWO HOUSES.

During the night of January 10, the dual House having remained in continuous session, Messrs. Dunsmore and Douglass slept behind the Speaker's desk while the members maintained a constant vigilance to prevent either of the opposing factions securing any advantage over the other.

At 10 a. m. on Wednesday, January 11, both Houses were called to order, an adjournment was taken by each to complete the legislative day, and roll call immediately opened the second regular day of the session.

The only incident worthy of note was the adoption by the revolutionary Republican House of a concurrent resolution authorizing a committee consisting of two members of the Senate and three members of the House to wait on the Governor and State officials and inform them that the House and Senate were duly organized and ready to proceed with business.

This had been done on the preceding day by the Dunsmore house, and the matter of recognition of one or the other branches of the dual House was taken under advisement by the Executive.

By mutual consent there was a cessation of hostilities, the hope that a compromise satisfactory to all parties might be arrived at having sprung up. A committee of fifteen, consisting of five representatives of each of the political parties, met in conference, and pending its report both Houses adjourned until 9 a. m. on Thursday.

The Senate, meantime, had refrained from recognizing a messenger from either house.

The tenacity with which the conspirators adhered to their plan of precipitating violence was shown by their organ, which, on the morning of this day, declared it to be the plan of the People's party to obtain recognition by the Governor and the Senate and then throw out the Republicans by force. If proceedings are commenced in the Supreme Court, added the Capital, they will impeach one of the Judges and run things to suit themselves.

The following paragraph, calculated to widen the breach between the two houses and prevent an amicable settlement of the difficulty, appeared in the same paper:

Jerry Simpson said last evening that every able-bodied Populist in Kansas would be called out if necessary to take forcible possession of the House.

On the following morning was published an appeal, signed by A. A. Harris and J. B. Crouch, leaders of the self-styled Stalwart Democracy of Kansas, and generally recognized as assistant Republicans. It was addressed to "Hon. T. G. Chambers, Stephen Meagher and Joe Rosenthal, House of Representatives, Topeka, Kan.," and urged them to unite their energies and action with the Republicans.

In servile obedience to this Stalwart ukase, Messrs. Meagher, Chambers and Rosenthal on this day (January 12) signified their allegiance to their masters by taking their seats with the Republicans.

On the same day the Reed rule was adopted by the Populist House and thirteen Republicans were reported by the clerk as present and participating in the proceedings. The great sensation of the day came, however, when at 5:20 p. m., several hours after the three Democrats had so ignomin-

iously surrendered to the Republican conspirators, the official recognition of the House presided over by Mr. Dunsmore came from Governor Lewelling.

The message was brought to the hall by the governor's private secretary, Major Fred J. Close, and was by the chief clerk read to Speaker Dunsmore of the legal House, amid the most perfect quiet. It was as follows.

TOPEKA, Kan., Jan. 12, 1893.

J. M. Dunsmore, Speaker of the House of Representatives:

In answer to your communication sent me January 10, 1893, notifying me that the House was organized with J. M. Dunsmore as Speaker, R H. Semple as Speaker pro tem., Jen C. Rich Chief Clerk, L. F. Dio a Sergeant-at-Arms, and ready for business, I desire to say that I will communicate with you later in writing.

L. D. LEWELLING, Governor.

The reading of this message was followed by the wildest cheering from the Populist members and their friends, as it was thought all controversy concerning the organization was thus brought to an end, and that all danger of serious trouble was happily averted.

At 6:30 p. m. by amicable agreement both Houses adjourned until 9:30 a. m. on Friday.

In the Capital of January 13 appeared the following double-leaded call for "A Public Meeting":

It has been suggested that it would be well for the citizens of Topeka, regardless of party, to call a mass meeting to protest against the use of gubernatorial power aiding the revolutionary spirit now rampant on the Populist side of the lower House. The people of Kansas should meet and discuss the situation in every city and village in the State. Let the protests of the people be made for the sake of the credit and good name of the State. The people have a right to protest against anarchy and revolution now threatened. Let us have a meeting in Topeka.

In the face of the peace and quiet prevailing in Representative Hall, of the negotiations that had been entered upon for a settlement of all differences, and of the recognition twelve hours before of the Dunsmore House by Governor Lewelling, a more incendiary and dangerous utterance could scarcely have been published. It reveals the alarm of the corporation conspirators lest their plans would be frustrated and demonstrates plainly the persistent and insidious effort they were making to bring about au open collision, which they designed to use as a cover for more desperate measures to overthrow the legally-constituted authorities and reverse the mandate of the people of Kausas as expressed at the polls in November.

OVERTURES FOR PEACE.

REPRESENTATIVE COBUN'S, PROPOSITION—FORMAL RECOGNITION OF THE POPULIST HOUSE BY THE SENATE—"THE COURTS WILL TAKE A HAND IN THE GAME"—NO HOPE OF AGREEMENT.

Friday, January 13, was a day of comparative quiet. On the whole, it saw the position of the Populist Representatives materially strengthened. The papers in the mandamus proceedings instituted in the Supreme Court Thursday evening by Speaker Douglass to compel Secretary of State Osborn to deliver to the Republican House all the depositions and other documents in the contests pending for seats in the House were withdrawn early in the morning by the Republican attorneys, it being discovered that they had already been turned over to the legal House, and that the attempt to compel an officer to deliver papers that were not in his possession was a farce. During the sessions of the dual House the floor and galleries were packed to suffocation, as public interest in the struggle had been roused to the highest pitch. There was no clash between the contending forces.

In the Senate, President Daniels recognized Benjamin C. Rich as Chief Clerk of the House of Representatives, and on appeal the Chair was sustained in such recognition by a vote of twenty-three to sixteen. Several of the Senators filed protests and a general protest was filed by the Republicans.

The Republican members of the conference committee reported that all attempts to bring about a settlement had been unsuccessful.

The formal recognition of the ⊥opulist House by the Senate as the legal House of Representatives of the State of Kansas came on the fifth legislative day, January 14, when, after a heated debate, the concurrent reso lution previously passed by the House was adopted by a vote of 22 to 17. Senators Rodgers and Householder were appointed as members of the joint committee, and immediately left the Senate chamber with the members of the House to wait upon the Governor, and announce that both Houses were organized and ready for business.

On their return they reported that the Governor would transmit his message to both Houses on Tuesday morning at 10 o'clock.

And so the week closed with the House over which Mr. Dunsmore presided recognized by the Governor and the Senate, and in both law and equity the legal House of Representatives of the State of Kansas. And on this very day it is recorded by no less authority than the Capital, there was made

"A proposition for a peaceable settlement of the controversy between the Populists and Republicans, which gives more promise of success than any that has yet been made. It came from the Populist House, and looks to an adjustment of the difficulty without the interference of outside influence."

The proposition referred to was presented by Representative Cobun, a Populist, and adopted by the legal House, being in the form of a resolution, as follows:

Resolved, That in the interest of harmony and the hope of a peaceable settlement of present difficulties now pending in the House, that the House do now adjourn to meet at the hour of 4 o'clock, Monday, January 16, 1893, with the mutual understanding that no persons shall be admitted to the floor or galleries except the members and those having contests.

In offering this resolution Mr. Cobun said: "We have been riding upon the waves of excitement here for nearly one week. I express the sentiment of a large majority of our side of the House when I say we want to settle this difficulty; we do not intend to deprive you of the opposite side of the House of your rights, nor do we propose that you shall deprive us of our rights. I say that this can be settled, if we can get together free from all outside influences: clear this floor of all persons except members and those who have contests and if we can, find some peaceable way out of this trouble. I believe the whole State of Kansas wants to see just such a settlement. This is no time to publish resolutions calculated to inflame the people, but it is a time for calm thought."

Mr. Hoch, of the Republican House, said: "I am in perfect accord with the remarks from the member on the other side. I have come to believe that we are as fine a body of men gathered here as could be gathered from the State of Kansas. Had these differences been left alone to the members of the floor, gathered here as a legislative family with no outside interference, these differences would long since have been settled. When in the spirit of friendliness we shall meet here to settle these things among ourselves, we will, in my opinion, succeed."

It is further recorded that "the resolution was adopted and the House adjourned."

It is evident that at this time, in the absence of anger and partisan excitement, Mr. Hoch, who was the recognized leader of the Republican House, did not regard the members of the rival House as "Anarchists," 'Revolutionists" or "military satraps."

And the way the party organ aided in furthering the design to avoid "the interference of outside influence' was by descanting in its Sunday morning issue on "the utterly lawless methods adopted by the Populists," in condemning "the military control of the House,' in publishing a manifesto from Speaker Douglass and the Republican House in which the Governor was denounced as "a violator of right and justice,' and the Populist members as "usurpers attempting to hold seats in the Legislature in violation of the Constitution of this State," and appealing to "the patriotic people of Kansas," a very wide range of "outside influence," not to lay at their doors "the bleeding corpse of liberty, and pointing to enthroned usurpation and revolution, exclaim: 'you men are responsible for this.'"

Of a truth, in those days the jewel of consistency was in the possession of neither the Republican press, nor the Republican legislators.

In this same Sunday morning paper appeared, as a further evidence of the desire of the conspirators of whom its editor was the spokesman to meet the Populists half way in their effort to bring order out of chaos, the fourth installment of that driveling idiocy and, illogical hogwash known as "Letters to Governor Lewelling,"—two columns of "insult added to injury," with this gratuitous suggestion:

"The Ben Rich House may continue to play at lawmaking, but *the courts will take a hand in the game* before this thing goes much farther."

The italics are our own. Even while ostensibly negotiating for a peaceful settlement, the Capital showed the hand of the conspirators and foreshadowed that which ultimately came to pass, when the courts did take a hand in the game with a vengeance.

This is a fair sample of the manner in which were received all the overtures for peace made by the representatives of the People's party. There could be but one result expected in the face of such downright duplicity and treachery. It was announced in the very next issue of the Capital, which had gone out of its way to interfere where "outside interference" was officially deprecated by both sides of the dual House.

The rival Houses of Representatives are as far apart as they ever were, and the outlook for an amicable adjustment of differences is far from encouraging. * * * At this time it looks very much as if there would be two Houses throughout the session.

This was literally "the whole thing in a nutshell," and for it the Capital and the clique of conspirators representing the railroad and bank corporations in the political arena are responsible.

On Monday, January 10, the House met as provided for in Mr. Coburn's resolution, and on motion agreed to hold an informal meeting with the view, if possible, to devise some means to bring about a peaceful solution of the existing difficulties. This meeting resulted in the appointment of a committee of three from each side, which committee immediately went into a conference, which resulted as follows:

After carefully examining all points in dispute, the committee on behalf of the Populist House presented the following proposition to the committee representing the Republican House:

John Seaton, Col. A. Warner and J. A. Troutman:

We submit the following proposition: That Judge Foster, Judge Horton and Judge Allen be agreed upon as a commission of three before whom all contest cases shall be submitted for settlement, and whose decision shall be final in all cases. This proposition was unanimously rejected by the Republican committee.

The committee on the part of the Populists then proposed to drop Judge Foster and allow the two remaining judges to select the third one. This proposition was also rejected.

The committee then adjourned to meet on the following morning, at which time it was decided by common consent that further negotiations were unnecessary, as there was no hope of agreement, and the committee so reported.

The Populist committee of conference in this instance consisted of M. W. Cobun, W. H. Ryan and W. M. Campbell.

TWO IMPORTANT ACTS.

THE REPUDLICANS GO THROUGH THE FARCE OF ELECTING A STATE PRINTER—THE POPULIST HOUSE AND SENATE IN JOINT SESSION ELECT JOHN MARTIN UNITED STATES SENATOR—LEGALITY OF THIS ACTION UNQUESTIONED.

On Tuesday, January 17, the House presided over by George L. Douglass, together with fifteen Republican Senators, held an alleged joint session and inaugurated the farce of attempting to elect a State Printer, but without the ability to secure a majority among their own number for any one of the candidates, although the caucus nominee received 79 of the 83 votes, legal or illegal, held necessary to a choice. The second day's balloting resulted in a similar manner, and the whole subject may here be disposed of in a few words.

The Populist Senate and House refrained from holding a new election for State Printer until later in the same month, when E. H. Snow was re-elected. The fact that he to-day retains that position, and that there is no pretense of questioning his authority, is one of the strong proofs of the validity of the action of the Populist House, and also of the impotency of the rival house to successfully attack Mr. Snow's claim.

Another striking proof of the inconsistency of Republican pretensions and Republican action, or rather inaction, is seen in the fact that Hon. John Martin, who was elected at a joint session of the Senate and the Populist House to be United States Senator from Kansas for the next two years, was duly admitted to a seat in the Senate of the United States and is to-day participating in the work of that most dignified and august of American legislative bodies. Now does any Republican, much less a Democrat or Populist, entertain the slightest idea that Senator Martin will ever be unseated, or that the so-called contest instituted by J. W. Ady, the choice of an alleged joint session of the two branches of the Legislature similar to that which attempted to elect a State Printer, will ever amount to anything more than a formal compliance with the instructions given the Senate Committee appointed to investigate the election in the Kansas Legislature?

Did the Republicans regard as sound the subsequent decision of the Supreme Court in the Gunn case, is it at all likely that they would permit the election of Senator Martin by the Populist House and State Senate to stand? And if the action of the House in thus electing a United States Senator is invulnerable to attack, wherein did the status of the Populist House change in the eyes of the law, save by the decision of the Supreme Court just referred to, and which has from the day on which the opinion was handed down by Chief Justice Horton been the subject of the severest censure and most scathing criticism?

The fact is that the decisions of the Supreme Court of Kansas in the mandamus proceedings instituted by Rice and Rosenthal, in which it was held unlawful to go behind the returns of a canvassing board, and in which the well known principle that the House is the exclusive judge of the election and qualifications of its members was reaffirmed by this court, together with the recognition of the Populist House by the Governor and the co-ordinate branch of the Legislature. the Senate, under the above law, established conclusively and irrevocably the legality of the body presided over by Mr. Dunsmore as the constitutional House of Representatives of the State of Kansas.

It is because of this that two of the most important acts of the Legislature of 1893—the re-election of State Printer Snow and the election of Hon. John Martin as United States Senator, remain virtually unquestioned, and will so remain for all time to come.

―――――

THE ELECTIONS COMMITTEE.

THE DECISION IN "THE POSTMASTER CASES" SUSTAINED BY HIGH AUTHORITY—THE GRAY COUNTY CASES—SEVEN POPULIST CONTESTANTS SEATED.

In both Houses Committees on Elections were appointed by their respective Speakers on Tuesday, January 17, and the work of investigating the contest cases was actually commenced. The Populist Elections committee, of which Representative A. H. Lupfer was Chairman, consisted of five People's party members and two Republicans. The latter, however, refused to act, maintaining that the Douglass pretended house was the constitutional body.

The first report of this committee was on the Coffey county contest, and recommended that O. M. Rice be given the seat instead of T. O. Ballinger, Republican, on the ground that the County Canvassing Board of Coffey county intentionally falsified the returns, and represented to the State Canvassing board that there was a tie between Rice and Ballinger, when; as a matter of fact, Rice had one majority, and was entitled to the

certificate. This case has been fully explained in the chapter on Supreme Court proceedings,

Nick Kline, certificated republican member from Jackson county, whose case has also been explained in detail in connection with the mandamus proceedings, was deposed because of the omission of the city of Holton, in the Legislative act of 1890, from the Thirty-eighth Representative district.

The contest in the Seventy-seventh district, Reno county, was similar to that in the Jackson county. The County Canvassing Board found that J. W. Dix (Republican) received 1,535 votes, and W. H. Mitchell (Populist) 1,511 votes. The committee recommended that the votes cast in the city of Nickerson be not counted, that city not appearing in the apportionment act. This gave Dix but 1,262 votes, while Mitchell had 1,394 votes. The committee, in its report, said:

County Commissioners and other canvassing boards ought to be advised in the most emphatic manner that their duties are purely ministerial—that they are to count and canvass the returns as made to them by the proper officers; that they do not possess any of the powers of a contest court, much less any legislative power. It has been said, and will likely be said again, that the votes canvassed by the commissioners in excess of those returned from the several precincts constituting the districts as defined by law, were cast in territory which ought to have been included in said districts respectively. If such should prove to be the case the question is one for the Legislature to determine, and not for the County Commissioners. In view of the facts in the case the acts of the Commissioners were illegal and wholly unauthorized, and their illegal acts confer no right or authority to office: and all votes added by the County Commissioners as canvassers to those actually cast in the district created by law should be rejected and disregarded.

In the case of Fox Winnie against S. F. Danner, the sitting member from the Thirtieth Senatorial District, composed of McPherson and Harvey Counties, the causes alleged by the contestant were bribery, fraud and corruption on the part of judges of elections: malconduct, fraud and corruption on the part of the board of county canvassers; not eligible to office: illegal votes; errors and mistakes on the part of judges of election and board of canvassers; intimidation.

With reference to the case of John Morrison, who claimed a seat in the House as a Representative for the One Hundred and Twenty-second Representative District. Gray County, his petition alleging that frauds had been committed in several of the townships at the election held for Representatives on the 8th day of November, the committee sent a subpœna to the County Clerk of Gray County, requiring him to bring before the committee the poll-books and the package of tickets returned by the judges of election from certain townships to him as County Clerk. This was done, and the committee counted the votes or ballot so produced, and found that the judges of election had fraudulently counted eighteen blank ballots as if they had been cast for Mr. Douglass, and had counted five ballots for Ora B. Douglass, the Republican candidate, which had actually been cast for Mr. Morrison, thus giving Mr. Douglass twenty-three more votes than he received, and depriving Mr. Morrison of five votes actually cast for him, making a difference of twenty-eight votes. The County canvass gave Mr. Douglass fifteen majority, when in fact Mr. Morrison had thirteen majority and was honestly elected. Upon finding these facts the House justly gave the seat to Mr. Morrison.

The report of the Committee on Elections included the evidence and legal argument and precedents justifying the decision of the House, in which the following cases in which the contestees were filling the positions of federal postmasters at the time of their election:

First district, Doniphan county—J. M. Howard vs. James A. Campbell.

Thirty-fifty district, Shawnee county—D. M. Howard vs. A. C. Sherman.

Ninty-ninth district, Ness county—I. N. Goodwin vs. R. O. Elting.

One hundred and twentieth district, Grant county—F. B. Brown vs. Peter Bowers.

With reference to these "postmaster cases," says the official statement of the organization of the House, as found in the House journal (pages 140 to 146), which statement was introduced in the form of a resolution by Mr. Wright, of Edwards, it should be remembered that section 5 of article 2 of the constitution of this State provides that no member of Congress or officer of the United States shall be eligible to a seat in the Legislature. The Supreme Court of California, in the case of Searey vs. Grow, 15 Cal. 117, in passing on a similar proposition, in which one Grow was elected to the office of sheriff, and at the time of the election held the United State office of postmaster, but resigned prior to his being qualified and entering upon the duties of his office, the court used the following language in defining the word "eligible:" "We understand the word 'eligible' to mean capable of being chosen—the subject of selection and choice. The people in this case were clothed with this power of choice; their selection of the candidate gave him all the claim to the office which he has. His title to the office comes from their designation of him. But they could not designate or choose a man not eligible—that is not capable of being selected They might select any man they choose, subject only to this *exception*, that the man they selected was capable of taking what they had the power to give. We do not see how the fact that be became capable of taking that office after they had exhausted their power of choice, can avail the appellant. We do not see how it can be argued that, by the acts of the candidate, the votes which were ineffectual when cast, because not given for a qualified candidate, became effectual to elect him to office."

It will be seen that the decision of the Elections Committee in the "postmaster cases" is sustained by high authority.

On Friday, January 20, the House, by a unanimous vote, adopted the report of the Elections Committee and seated the following members:

Doniphan County—J. W. Howard (Populist) seated in place of J. A. Campbell (Republican).

Coffey County—O. M. Rice (Populist) in place of T. C. Ballinger (Republican).

Jackson County—Ed. Shellabarger (Populist) in place of Nick Kline (Republican).

Reno County—W. H. Mitchell (Populist) in place of J. W. Dix (Republican).

Shawnee County—D. M. Howard (Populist) in place of A. C. Sherman (Republican).

Ness County—I. N. Goodwin (Populist) in place of Richard O. Elting (Republican).

Grant County—F. B. Brown (Populist) in place of Peter Bowers (Republican).

THE MORRIS COUNTY CASE.

FRAUDULENT CONDUCT OF THE JUDGES OF
ELECTION IN OHIO TOWNSHIP—THEIR CON-
DUCT STRONGLY CENSURED BY THE HOUSE.

On Saturday, January 21, the Committee
on Elections submitted to the House a report, which was adopted, recommending
that W. H. White, Populist, be seated as the
member from Morris County, instead of H.
E. Richter, Republican. Richter's majority, according to the returns of the Canvassing Board was eight, but the committee,
upon fully investigating the case, found that
Mr. White was elected by a majority of
fifteen. It was found that seven non-resi-
dents had voted; that, in Ohio Township,
two ballots—one Democratic and one Pro
hibition—were rejected, upon each of which
was a vote for White; that C. L. Thomas,
one of the Judges of Election in Ohio Township, substituted a number of Republican
ballots for Populist ballots, this number
being not less than seven, nor more than
twenty, etc. As this was a peculiarly aggra-
vated case we quote from the report of the
committee:

Respecting the fraudulent conduct of the
Judges of Election, the testimony shows,
that at the November election held in Ohio
Township, C. L. Thomas, D. Brooks and H.
H. Bailey were the Judges of Election. Mr.
Thomas took the tickets from the box, and
handed most of them to Brooks to read, and
Bailey strung them. During the counting
of the votes, ballots "were lying all over the
counter" where the ballot box stood, and
Thomas had ballots in his hand from time
to time which he had taken from the table.
He was seen to fold up such ballots, and his
actions attracted such attention that he was
openly accused of changing ballots, that is,
substituting tickets taken from the table for
those taken out of the ballot box. Mr. C.
H. Titus testified that he was present during
the counting of the votes, and that Mr.
Bailey, one of the judges of the election,
openly charged Mr. Thomas with changing
ballots, using the following words:
"Here, Thomas, you must stop that changing of ballots; *that is two or three I have
seen you change.*"

Mr. G. W. Campbell testifies to the same

or a similar transaction during the same
counting. He says the following colloquy
took place between Bailey and Campbell:
Bailey—I want you to quit changing those
tickets.

Thomas—I am not changing them.
Bailey—You did; I saw you; there is another [ticket] lying there, folded up.

Mr. Campbell states that Thomas hesi-
tated awhile, and then he said he had
"folded up the ballot to throw at the boys."
Mr. Campbell also testifies that the ballot
which Bailey had charged Thomas with substituting for a ballot taken from the ballot-
box "was a Republican ticket," and was
counted.

Mr. Bailey, one of the judges of said election, also testified. He says that Mr. Thomas
did change the ballots, and the remarkable
story of fraud and corruption which he tells
should be repeated in his own words, that
the people, not merely of the Fifty-seventh
District, but of the whole State, may understand how they are robbed and defrauded of
their votes, and how the ballot box is robbed
by men who pose as its protectors. Mr.
Bailey says that he was sitting with his face
toward Thomas, having his hat down over
his eyes, but so adjusted that he could plainly see both of the hands of Thomas, and
watched Thomas' movements. We quote
from Mr. Bailey's testimony, as follows:
"Thomas took the tickets out of the box,
Brooks read them, and I strung them. * *
* The first thing that attracted my attention, he was taking the tickets out of the box
long before it was necessary, then holding
them down in front of him under the edge
of the table and opening them enough so
that he could see the heading of them; then
he would fold them back, and throw under
the right hand; then he would put
his right hand under the left,
and was working with the tickets
until Mr. Brooks would get ready for it.
Then he would unfold the ticket and hand
it to Mr. Brooks, Then as soon as Mr.
Brooks commenced to read the ticket he
would take another out of the box, and go
through the same motion as he did before,
with part of the tickets. I noticed him do
this for four, five or six times. The desk
the ballot box stood on was about four
inches lower than the table the clerks worked
upon, and projected over the table the ballot box stood on about three inches. There
were two tickets lying under this projection,
folded up the same as ballots in the box. He
took a ticket out of the ballot box, held it
down in front of him under the edge of the
table, and opened it enough to examine the
heading, placed it in his right hand as before, put it under the other hand and worked
it under the same as he had before. His left
hand was within an inch or two of those
two tickets under the projection. Then he
worked the ticket that he took out of the
box back under his hand, and took one of
the other tickets that lay there. Then he

unfolded that ticket and handed it to Mr. Brooks to read. The ticket that he took out of the box at that time was a People's party ticket. The one he took in its place was a Republican ticket. The way I know that the first one was a People's party ticket was that I saw the heading of it, and of the one that he put in its place being a Republican ticket I saw it and heard Mr. Brooks read it, "When I discovered what I have just related, I demanded of Mr. Thomas to hand Mr. Brooks the ticket he took out of the box. He said he did. I told him he did not, for I saw him change it. He said that he did not change it. I told him he need not deny it, as I saw him do it. He further denied but would give no explanation. * * * He did not get out of humor, but simply denied it. * * * I presume he must have changed seven or eight from the first time I saw him working with them. He might have changed fifteen or twenty before I commenced noticing him."

Mr. Bailey says that other persons had the same opportunity to observe Mr. Thomas as he had. Messrs. W. Myers, Henry Myers, G. B. Campbell and R. H. Bogle were also in the room, and they testified as to the conduct of Mr. Thomas during the counting of the votes. From the whole testimony your committee find that Mr. Thomas was guilty of the most flagrant violation of the provisions of section 20 of the election law, which requires that the ballots be taken out one at a time, by one of the judges, who shall himself read the names thereon aloud, before another ballot shall be touched. He did this for a while, and then, instead of reading the ballots himself, he passed them to Mr. Brooks to read, and spent his time in stealing tickets and examining them secretly, and changing tickets which had never been cast for ballots which had actually been voted. The animus of the man is shown by the testimony of G. W. Campbell who describes Mr. Thomas' conduct while he (Thomas) was reading the ballot. Mr Campbell says:

"During the first part of the count Mr. Thomas appeared to be well pleased. The tickets were mostly all Republican at the time. He was gathering up handful of tickets and throwing them at the boys—reaching over and getting them off the table. He would, when he would get a Republican ticket, read it out very distinct; but when he would get a People's party ticket, he would read it with a whine. About the middle of the count, the People's party ticket commenced to gain, and came up within four or five of the Republican.

"Mr. Thomas commenced to get nervous, and would take a ticket out of the box before Mr. Brooks got through reading the previous one. After a while, as soon as he handed Brooks a ticket, he would take out another and open it and look at it. He would take them down on his lap and appear to be opening them. After he had taken down from fifteen to twenty, as near as I could tell, Mr. Bailey made the charge."

Your committee respectfully submit, that the testimony clearly shows that Mr. Thomas should be prosecuted and convicted of a felony, for violating the provisions of section 219 of the act relating to crimes and punishments, and that if the proper officers fail to bring him to justice, they will be grossy derelect in the performance of an important public duty

---

KIOWA COUNTY BRIBERY CASE.

UNBLUSHING ATTEMPTS OF THE REPUBLICAN CANDIDATE TO BUY HIS WAY INTO THE HOUSE—A REMEDY FOR TRICKERY, FRAUD AND CORRUPTION SUGGESTED.

On February 2 the House adopted the report and resolutions submitted by the Elections committee in the contest of J. W. Hair vs. J. W. Davis, for the seat of Representative from the Ninety-fourth Representative District, embracing the County of Kiowa, and J. W. Hair was duly sworn and took his seat as a member. This was what is known as the "Kiowa County bribery case," and reveals another phase of Republican manipulation when votes are badly wanted.

By the returns in the office of the Secretary of State, Davis was shown to have received, as a candidate on the Republican ticket, 401 votes, and J. W. Hair, as a candidate on the Populist ticket, 369 votes—thus showing a majority for Davis of thirty-two votes. There were no other candidates for the office. In the statement and notice of contest filed by Mr. Hair, it was charged, among other things, that Davis had given some of the electors who voted for him, and had offered to give to sundry other electors voting at the same election, bribes and rewards, in money and other things of value, for the purpose of procuring his election to said office, which grounds of contest were duly verified by affidavit. Mr. Davis ignored the notice of the committee and remained away, whereupon the investigation was proceeded with in his absence.

R. 3.Treadway, a resident of Greensburg. in Kiowa county, testified that on the 8th of November last, as he was going along the street in Greensburg, he saw standing in front of a store, Mr. J. W. Davis, who engaged the witness in conversation, and, stepping up to him, pushed into his vest pocket a small parcel of rolled up paper, and at the same time handed witness a republican ticket, on which was printed the name of said J. W. Davis as a candidate for Representative of said Ninety-fourth district, and said to the witness, "Let's go vote." The witness started with Davis toward the election polls, Davis leading the way; in that relative position, the witness put the ticket which he had so received from Davis into his pocket, and took therefrom a People's party ticket which did not contain the name of said Davis, and deposited the People's party ticket in the ballot box, is his vote at that election. Shortly afterwards the witness examined the parcel which Davis had thrust into his pocket, and found it to be money,—a five dollar bill—rolled up. The witness further testified that when he had voted Davis at once indicated symptoms of anger toward him; that it had been their custom to meet almost daily, and Davis was very cordial toward him, and would come across the room to shake hands with him, but now their relations were entirely changed; that Davis had, since the election, sought to avoid him, and would go around a block to keep out of his way; that since the election the witness and Davis had had one conversation only, and that was while they were on the cars together while the witness was coming to testify in this case, in obedience to the subpœna served on him. Davis came to witness on the car and asked him where he was going, and what his purpose was; and after the witness had answered him, Davis retorted: "You will not get back in ten years." The witness further said, that at the time Davis gave him the money. Davis owed him nothing, and there was no reason why Davis should give him the money, and the witness had no other thought or understanding from what was said or done at the time but that the money was given him (the witness) to vote for him

(Davis) as such candidate for said office. The committee found that Davis did offer and give the said five dollars to said witness as a bribe to procure his election.

The committee also examined John Derly, who testified that he had for six years last past been a resident of Kiowa county, living on his farm, some twenty miles northeast of Greensburg; that J. W. Davis came to his farm about one week before the general election in November and offered to the witness $2 to vote for him and work for his election at the polls. The witness answered that he had no capacity for electioneering, and could not do it, and would not take the $2; thereupon Davis offered him the $2 to go to the polls and vote for him on election day, and, holding the money, the two-dollar bill, between his thumb and finger, thrust it into the witness' vest pocket. The witness took the money out and gave it back to Davis, saying: "I don't want anything in that way." The committee found the fact to be, that Davis did at the time and place stated, give and offer to Joseph Derley $2 as a bribe to procure his election to the office of Representative from that district.

Upon the strength of these facts the Elections committee, in its report to the House (House Journal, page 163) found that J. W. Davis was disqualified from holding said office, and adds:

Three other witnesses have been duly subpœnaed at the request of the contestant in this case who have refused to answer the command of the subpœna, viz.: Frank Leard, David Bright and Willis L. Smith, the last of whom has given his voluntary affidavit of another like act, showing a constitutional disqualification, but we believe that no good purpose can be served by a further postponement of this case to obtain additional evidence of these matters, sufficient proof having been already developed to demand the action of this House, and to open the way for fuller investigation in the proper criminal courts. The language of the constitution applicable to this case is as follows:

"Every person who shall have given or offered a bribe to procure his election shall be disqualified from holding office during the term for which he may have been elected."

So far as declaring J. W. Davis to be disqualified to hold the office of Representative from the Ninety-fourth District, our duty is clear; but this brings us to the question, whether J. W. Hair, the only opponent of Davis at the election, and who received thirty-two votes less than Davis, should be seated as the Representative of that district instead of Davis. We should approach this question with a less degree of confidence were it not for the legislative precedent which was established in Kansas as early as 1865.

In the contest case then before the Legislature from Woodson county, of Joel Moody, contestant, against Jonathan Foster, contestee, made upon the ground that Foster was ineligible because of his being a Postmaster by appointment under the United States, Foster, the Postmaster, was ousted, and Moody, who had eleven votes less than Foster, was seated. The case was a vigorously contested one, and the decision was sustained by a vote of fifty-nine yeas against eleven nays, and there was numbered in the majority many of the very most eminent and able awyers who have adorned the history of the state.

It would be difficult to find a substantial basis for a distinction between the case in 1865, above referred to, and the one now under consideration. A general statement of the authorities respecting the seating of the minority candidate will be found in the report which was submitted to the House by this committee on January 19, and need not here be repeated. Many cases may be found decided by the courts of this country with respect to offices not legislative, wherein the declaration of the qualification of the incumbent merely creates a vacancy and re quires a new election or appointment. There is substantial justice in saying, that a candidate or constituency which is defeated by bribery on the part of the opposing party ought not so to be defeated. Our constitution provides that questions of the election, returns and qualifications of legislative officers shall not be subject to the decisions of the courts nor bound by their precedents. A rule which would be right with respect to other offices might be unjust and wrong when applied to legislative offices. A member of the Legislature cannot be appointed. The brief session of the Legislature may terminate before a new election could be held. A district ought not to be unrepresented. The whole matter is designedly left to the exclusive decision of the respective houses.

Therefore, the committee recommended that J. W. Hair be declared entitled to represent the Ninty-fourth legislative district, embracing the county of Kiowa, in the Legislature of Kansas, which recommendation was adopted.

THE REMEDY PROPOSED.

At the conclusion of the resolution introduced by Mr. Wright, of Edwards County, January 27, to officially settle the facts relating to the organization of the House, etc., was appended the following:

Resolved, That, to avoid a reoccurrence of the possibility of a like controversy in the future, that it is the sense of this House,

that section 8 of article 2 of the constitution, which provides that each House shall be the judge of the election returns and qualifications of its own members, (which though handed down to us as emblematic of the great fight between the commons and the crown, is not adapted to the needs of to-day,) be so amen ed as to permit the settlement of all contests of members of the Legislature prior to the time set for their *convening,* leading to which object a joint resolution has been introduced in the House proposing an amendment to section 8, article 2, of the constitution, so that said section may read as follows:

"SEC. 8. A majority of each House shall constitute a quorum. Each House shall establish its own rules, and all contests as to the election, returns and qualifications of the members of either House shall be determined in the county or district in which such election was held, in such manner as the Legislature shall provide."

We, therefore, the Representatives of the several districts, the numbers of which are set opposite our respective names, appealing to the Supreme Judge of the world for the rectitude of our intentions, do hereby solemnly publish the facts hereinbefore stated to be a true history of the organization of the House of Representatives, and the rights for maintaining the same, and hereby *challenge all statements to the contrary.*

It is not necessary to burden this record further with details of the corrupt and fraudulent methods to which the Republican party, during the campaign of 1892, resorted to perpetuate its power in Kansas. The report of the Elections Committee of the Populist House, in each of the contest cases commenced, was very full and complete, has been published in other form, and is accessable to those curious to follow the Republican plot through all its intricacies and ramifications. These committee reports, as spread upon the House Journal, reveal a degree of recklessness and criminality that is incomprehensible. The proofs are unimpeachable, the arguments unanswerable. Enough has been already referred to or quoted to convey a fair idea of the whole From the beginning of the campaign in the spring of 1892, until November 8, when the struggle ended at the polls, fraud, misrepresentation and utter disregard of all the principles of good government and all the rights of a sovereign people marked the course of the then dominant party. From November 8 until the date of the organization of the Legislature, the plans of the conspirators continued to develop daily, until they culminated in the revolution that divided the House of Representatives, blocked legislation, engendered partisan bitterness and strife, paralyzed temporarily all business in the State, and drew upon Kansas the astonished and contemptuous gaze of the whole world.

Of the corruption of men in high places, suspicion and certainty became inextricably mixed, the confidence of the people in their rulers was shaken and distrust rapidly developed into bitter resentment and open revolt, the supporters of corporate greed and tyranny as against the people and the commonwealth being in the end deposed from power and ignominiously turned down.

THRUST AND PARRY.

SPEAKER DUNSMORE INSISTS ON GETTING DOWN TO BUSINESS AND DOING SOMETHING FOR THE PEOPLE—SPEAKER DOUGLASS TEMPORIZES—HIS EVASIVE AND INSOLENT LETTER.

The events of the last ten days of January may be disposed of in a single paragraph. They included the election of Hon. John Martin as United States Senator, the re-election of E. H. Snow as State Printer, the visit to the Populist House of General Weaver, late People's party candidate for President, and other matters concerning which there is no controversy, though each was in itself of surpassing importance and interest at the time. During this period there was a growing feeling of disquietude and apprehension. All the overtures made to the Republicans for an amicable adjustment of differences, all appeals in behalf of peace, in the interests of the great commonwealth of Kansas, were alike unavailing. It was apparent that no proposition looking toward the settlement of mooted questions and the resumption of the business of the session, save one involving a complete surrender of rights by the Representatives of the people, would be considered by the House over which Geo. L. Douglass presided.

On Monday afternoon, January 30, Speaker Dunsmore transmitted to Speaker Douglass the following dignified, firm and business-like communication:

HOUSE OF REPRESENTATIVES, }
January 30, 1893. }

Hon. Geo. L. Douglass:

MY DEAR SIR:—As by the election of a United States Senator and State Printer the political reasons for obstruction in the House of Representatives no longer exist, I can conceive of no justifiable excuse in your refusal to recognize the authority of the executive, the Senate and the House of Representatives as now constituted: as a good lawyer, you are doubtless aware of the fact (if you have taken the trouble to inform yourself in relation to the facts and have consulted the journals of the House) that the present status between the executive and the legislative departments cannot be disturbed or annulled by the authority of any other tribunal, unless such tribunal should attempt to exercise a power not granted by the constitution and the law; and that the only possible reason for continued obstruction now existing, either to your party or personal to yourself, is the hope that by legal quibbling, the law's delay, and the favors of a partisan court, the Republican party, or at least its managers and Representatives of railroad and other corporate interests, may prevent the legislation that the people demand at our hands.

Every well informed man in Kansas is aware that the railroads and other corporate managers in this State are behind you, promoting and directing the action of your party to block the wheels of legislation, even going so far, I am informed by good authority, as to advance the pay you and other Republicans receive through one of the banks of this city, closely connected with certain railroad interests.

If, as you profess, you desire the legislation required by the debt burdened people of Kansas, is it not about time that you give evidence of that fact by recognizing the executive and legislative authorities now working in harmony? The experience of the last session should convince you that the legislation required can only be obtained by political union between the House of Representatives and the Senate. Upon this union depends, in a great measure, the possibility of legislation in favor of the World's Fair and many public institutions throughout the state, and especially along the line of railroad control.

Two years ago it was the Republican Senate against the opposition House. Many now desire a Republican House against an opposition Senate. In either case the result must be the same. As but a few committees have been appointed by me, opportunities still exist for an adjustment of the present trouble in a manner favorable to all concerned; and to that end I would be pleased to receive and consider any proposition you may deem proper to make, either verbally or in writing, that does not bring into question the integrity of the Legislature as now organized and the acts of the Executive in relation thereto.

If no such adjustment can be made we will be under the necessity of promptly proceeding to business without the valuable aid and advice of yourself and political friends, and let the people of Kansas judge between us.

With assurance of my personal regard, I am very truly yours, J. M. DUNSMORE, Speaker.

This communication was withheld by Speaker Douglass from the press, as well as from the pretended house, of which he was the head, until 2 p. m. on the following day, when it was read in the presence of the Republican House, together with the reply of Speaker Douglass, which was as follows:

HOUSE OF REPRESENTATIVES, TOPEKA, January 31, 1893.

HON. J. M. Dunsmore:

DEAR SIR:—I acknowledge the receipt of your letter of yesterday, and in reply thereto I beg leave to say:

On the 10th day of this month, after the majority of the duly elected members of the House of Representatives had organized the House and elected a speaker and other officers, a minority of fifty-eight members-elect proceeded to organize another body, which also calls itself the House of Representatives. As these fifty-eight members-elect were five less than a quorum, and absolutely powerless to perform any act, the official roll was obtained and there, in the broad daylight, before the eyes of hundreds, the names of ten members chosen by the people were scratched out and in their stead were inserted the names of ten other persons who were not elected, and some of whom had been defeated at the polls by majorities of 500 to 1,000 votes. This was done by Ben O. Rich, without any adjudication of the contests by any tribunal whatsoever, and upon the call of this forged roll, and with the aid of these ten persons (whose only claim to seats was that they had served notice of a contest upon the members whose election had been regularly ascertained and certified by the proper officers), the body over which you preside was organized.

The majority at its organization chose me as its Speaker, and of the members who participated in that day's proceedings sixty-four voted for me as Speaker and three others, on the 12th day of January, took their seats in the lawful House of Representatives, and have since uniformly adhered, and still do adhere to it as the only House of Representatives known to the constitution and the laws.

If the proceedings by means of which the body over which you preside was organized should ever be acquiesced in by the people of Kansas it would be the end of regular, orderly and constitutional government in this commonwealth.

The fact that the Governor and a majority in the Senate have so far succumbed to the pressure of party considerations as to countenance such a proceeding in no wise changes the fact, except as it intensifies the obligation and emphasizes the duty of all law-abiding citizens to protest against it. Such countenance by the executive and the Senate cannot annihilate or destroy the legal and constitutional House of Representatives, chosen by the people to do the people's will. The powers of the executive and the Senate are many and great, but the power to perform miracles is not one of them, and, despite all assertions to the contrary, it remains true that they are powerless either to create a majority out the minority or to destroy by their fiat constitutional and lawful body of the resentatives of the people.

I take issue with your assumption that the courts have no power to determine whether an alleged act of the Legislature was ever in fact passed by the Legislature of the State or by some other body. The prime duty of the courts, where the validity of a statute is called in question, is to ascertain whether the constitutional requirements have been observed in its passage; and if they find that, instead of such observance, the constitution has been trampled under foot and that the alleged act has not been passed by the lawful House but by an usurping body, it is the highest duty of the Court to so declare. Such declaration, far from being an evidence of partisanship, would be a mark of that integrity, fidelity and devotion to duty which characterizes the American judiciary.

It is true that the constitutional House of Representatives cannot legislate without the concurrence of the Senate, and it is equally true that the minority body over which you preside cannot effectually legislate even with such concurrence.

It is also apparent to every thinking man that any attempt to so legislate must, in the course of a few weeks' time, come under the final review of the courts, and if the determination by the courts of the questions involved should be in accordance with what I have no doubt to be the law, it will ultimately necessitate an extra session of the Legislature with the attendant expense and burden upon the people. Under such circumstances it would seem to be a part of wisdom for men desirous of the public good to make up a case for the highest court at the earliest possible moment and set the matter at rest within a few days' time.

The law will in the end prevail. No men are as yet above the law in Kansas, however much they may desire to be, and the law-abiding people of our State will in the long run sustain the public servant who, regardless of temporary and partisan considerations, respects and obeys the law. Regard for law is the bulwark of free institutions. If the law be defective, as some of our statutes unfortunately are, it is our duty as legislators not to over-ride and over-throw the law, but to patriotically set about remedying its defects.

Your intimation that, in defending the rights of the constitutional body, of which I am the Speaker, I may be influenced by personal motives, and that I desire to prevent legislation demanded by the people, is an unworthy imputation which I must leave those who know me best to answer. In like manner I notice, but pass without comment, the unworthy reflection upon the integrity and character of the Democratic and Republican members of the lawful House of Representatives involved in your assertion 'hat in this struggle for law and order they :e prompted and directed by the railroads and other corporations. You will yourself recognize the peculiar impropriety of this when I recall to you the fact that on the 12th day of this month, after conferring with many of the members of the House, I offered (in event of the then proposed adjustment of our difficulties) to give not only a large number of leading committees to the members of the People's party, but also to give them the Chairmanship and full control of the Railroad Committee.

I have always been ready and still am to confer with yourself or any member with a view to securing an honorable adjustment of the present difficulties, to the end that legislation may proceed. But any adjustment which involves assent to the extraordinary methods whereby the body over which you preside was organized is and will remain an impossibility.

The members of the lawful House of Representatives propose to maintain to the end the laws and constitution of Kansas. They are willing to negotiate upon matters of less moment, but they will never sacrifice their obligations to the State and the people they represent. World's Fair bills and other legislation are as much desired by them as by yourself, but beyond and above all else their duty is to preserve, to the full limit of their power, the principle of constitutional liberty which is now at stake.

: Let there be no misunderstanding, therefore, as to their position. With the best of personal feeling, I beg leave to assure you that the constitutional House of Representatives is here to perform the high duties entrusted to it by the people, and here it will remain. Very respectfully yours,

GEO. L. DOUGLASS, Speaker.

In reply to this manifesto of the Republican Speaker, to the reading of which Speaker Dunsmore had listened attentively, and which the Republicans endorsed by resolution, promising to stand by their leader to the end, Speaker Dunsmore, at its conclusion said: "In answer to my friend's communication I have only to say that actions speak louder than words."

ACTIVE HOSTILITIES.

CHIEF CLERK RICH, OF THE POPULIST HOUSE, ARRESTED BY REPUBLICAN DEPUTIES—A REMARKABLE SCENE ON KANSAS AVENUE—RICH RESCUED—OMINOUS THREATS—THE SHERIFF REFUSES THE GOVERNOR'S DEMAND FOR PROTECTION FOR MEMBERS OF THE POPULIST HOUSE—THE APPROPRIATION BILL SIGNED B' THE GOVERNOR—ARTZ CONFIRMED AS ADJUTANT GENERAL.

It would be strange, indeed, if, after s/ protracted and bitter a struggle on the par of the representatives of the People's party to maintain their legal rights, and the dogged determination of the Republican conspirators to accomplish their purpose, a permanent truce could have been established. The astonishing patience and forbearance of the Populists is alone to be credited with so long averting a collision, which their opponents more than once sought to force upon them, a fact which the lapse of time since the exciting events of this Legislative session serves but to bring out more prominently. Following the exchange of communications between the two Speakers related in the preceding chapter, there was a period of comparative quiet, and on the surface it appeared that the dead-lock would continue throughout the session.

It was, however, but the calm which precedes the storm. The clouds were already gathering, and the observant watcher knew the tempest would break before many days. In pursuance of the plan agreed upon by the Republican leaders, the crisis was to be brought about by harrassing the Populist House, the method of procedure being in. dicated by the following article in the *Capital* of January 19:

The next move on the part of the Republicans will probably be to prosecute Chief Clerk Ben Rich, of the Populist House, for forgery and mutilation of the official roll of the Secretary of State on the day of the organization of the Legislature. The chief conspirator in the organization of the illegal house was Mr. Rich. He took Secretary Osborn's official roll of members, and, erasing the names of ten Republican members, inserted the names of ten Populists and read them off as legally elected members of the Legislature. Good lawyers say that in doing this Mr. Rich was guilty of forgery of public records, and Speaker Douglass said yesterday he had no doubt proceedings would be commenced to punish him to the full extent of the law.

Editorially the same paper expressed the opinion that "the time has come to begin criminal proceedings against Ben Rich," and that "the spurious house created by Ben Rich should be brought to a halt in its reckless rebellion."

"It is no longer," continued this appeal to the conspirators, "a time for words and more words, but a time to act. In behalf of the State of Kansas, her constitution, her laws and her loyal people, the *Capital* demands that the law be vindicated without further delay by legal proceedings against the instigators of treason."

And again: "How long is this anarchy to continue Governor Lewelling? What is to be the end of this high-handed effrontery and lawlessness? Unless you retrace your steps and enforce the laws on the statute book which you have sworn to enforce you will stand convicted at the bar of public sentiment of violating your oath of office. So long as you continue your present lawless attitude you are a traitor to the constitution and laws of Kansas, to the people whose servant you are, and to your oath of office, and your conscience."

There was no material change in the attitude of the two Houses, nor any developments of great importance until Tuesday, February 14, the date which marked the culmination of events, and the beginning of active hostilities on the part of the Republican House, which continued its lawless occupancy of the hall, its annoyance of the legal House of Representatives, and its interference with the legislation demanded in the interests of the State.

The Populist House was at work all this time, and doing its best to bring order out of chaos, but it was beset with many difficulties. Every step was taken with the utmost caution and consideration for the law,

and the Republicans, becoming fearful lest they would after all be unable to win in the courts, where they proposed to attack the appropriation ordinance passed by the House and awaiting the concurrence of the Senate and the signature of the Governor, determined to delay no longer the consummation of their scheme to bring matters to a crisis. During the morning their plans were formulated and at noon acted upon, with the result of creating the wildest excitement and precipitating a conflict between the two sides, during which blow were exchanged and bad blood engender' that destroyed forever all hope of a p ful settlement of the contest.

Speaker *pro tem* Hoch, of the I of House, had been selected to hurl the brand into the ranks of the opposh rep- which he did by introducing a res providing for the arrest of Chief r Rich. He prefaced his resolution following significant remarks:

"MR. SPEAKER: I know of but two by which men settle or attempt to s disputes, when mutual efforts fail—ei a resort to a knock-down or to the cou The knock-down plan never settles a thing, except the relative brutishness of contestants. The courts were instituted settle disputes between men who car settle them themselves. To the courts issue must finally come. We can not a it, we can only delay it. And why lor delay it?"

His resolution was then carried to t reading clerk and presented to the House. It was as follows:

WHEREAS, One Ben C. Rich, for a number of days last past, and during the presen session of this, the House of Representatives, and in the presence of said House, has continually interrupted the regular proceedings of the House by loud and boisterous language and unlawful and unusual noises without legal excuse or justification, and without claim or pretense that the same was a part of or connected with the proceeding of the House of Representatives, and such conduct has been and still is being indulged and persisted in by said Ben C. Rich, in open, malicious, and willful defiance and derision of the rules and authority of the House of Representatives; and

WHEREAS, Such conduct has greatly interrupted and interfered with the transaction of public business by the House, and has impeded and still impedes necessary legislation in the interest of the people of the State of Kansas, thereby bringing the authority and dignity of the House of Representatives into disrepute: therefore be it

Resolved, That by the said action and conduct of the said Ben C. Rich, he has been and is guilty of contempt of this House and the Speaker is hereby authorized and directed to cause said Ben C. Rich to be forthwith arrested by the Sergeant-at-Arms and brought before the bar of this House, to show cause, if any he have, why he should not be punished for such contempt, and that said Ben C. Rich be held in custody by said Sergeant-at-Arms, subject to the further order of the House of Representatives.

Immediately after the adoption of this resolution Speaker Douglass directed the Sergeant-at-Arms to carry out the order of the House. As Sergeant-at-Arms Clevenger was absent from the city, three of his assistants, W. H. Young, of Wyandotte county; L. E. Clogston, of Greenwood county, and Jordan, of Rice county, were instructed to ⌐ .e the arrest, and left the House at once ⌐u search of Rich. They went direct to the Dutton House, where he was known to board, and found him in his room, with his wife and Representative D. M. Howard, of Shawnee county. The resolution of the Republican House was read to Mr. Rich, and he was informed that he was under arrest. He said he did not recognize the men who pre-tended to make the arrest as officers of the House of Representatives, such as they claimed to be, and declined to go with them. He added, however, that his duty would require him to go to the State house after dinner, and if they were disposed to wait they might go along. He even invited the pretended officers to dine with him, and one of them, Sergeant-at-Arms Young, accepted, while Jordan remained in the hotel office.

In the meantime news of this radical action on the part of the Republican House spread like wild-fire, and caused the most intense excitement on the streets, so that when Mr. Rich had completed his meal and announced his readiness to start for the Capitol, there was quite a throng of prominent men in front of the Dutton House. At 1:15 p. m. Mr. and Mrs. Rich left the hotel on foot for the State House, refusing to accept the proffer of a carriage from the alleged officers, though it was a bitter cold day and a chilling blast swept down the avenue. They were accompanied by a number of Mr.

Rich's Populist friends, including Hon. John W. Breidenthal, S. M. Scott, W. H. Ryan, Sergeant-at-Arms Dick, P. N. Gish, D. M. Howard, J. F. Willitts and Mr. Williams, of Fort Scott. The deputies followed in their train as near as possible to Mr. Rich, and thus they marched up Kansas avenue, presenting one of the most remarkable scenes ever witnessed in the Capital City.

By this time the Douglass House, after waiting more than an hour for the return of the deputies, had adjourned to 9 a. m. Wednesday and the majority of the officers and members were at the Copeland Hotel, their headquarters. When the Rich party reached Ninth street they were met by a messenger with an order for the deputies to bring Rich to the Copeland. The officers now pressed forward to take possession of their man, who was surrounded by a cordon of friends that was impenetrable. The deputies made a vigorous effort to break through, but met with a stout resistance and a struggle ensued, in which they were handled without gloves. Clogston made a desperate attempt to get at Rich, but Representative Ryan threw him violently to the ground and he, with the others, also recognizing that they had the worst of it, beat a retreat, while Rich and his friends proceeded to Representative Hall as if nothing had happened out of the usual order, arriving there a few minutes before 1:30 o'clock.

On entering the room Chief Clerk Rich was greeted with loud cheers from his friends, who had already gathered in large numbers, and at once became the hero of the hour. The House was called to order by Speaker Dunsmore, who said: "I regret very much the events which led to the exciting scenes of the past few hours. We have elected a legal majority of the House of Representatives and have passed ten bills which will become laws as soon as they have been signed by the Governor. If we are in the right, as we know we are, we will surely win and have nothing to fear. I wish to advise the members of the House to remain on the side of peace and order. If we are forced by circumstances to do so, we will press into service the forces of the state to maintain our constitutional rights. No matter what may be the excitement, retain your seats. This is simply a question as to whether the Santa Fe Railway Company and similar corporations are to control this State, or whether the people will do so."

The speaker was frequently interrupted by cheers. The regular order of business was then proceeded with and after the passage of a half dozen bills the following resolution was introduced by Representative Gest, of Jefferson, and adopted:

WHEREAS, An attempt has been made to arrest the Chief Clerk of this House by an organized mob calling themselves the Republican House of Representatives, but which we believe to be in reality the Santa Fe Railroad Company; therefore be it

Resolved, That we, the legally organized and constitutional House of Representatives, proclaim to the State of Kansas that the mob was foiled, and that our flag is still there.

Rich was closely guarded during the afternoon and evening, every precaution being taken to prevent a second attempt at arrest by the Republican officers.

The corporation conspirators were furious at being baffled in the effort to throw the Populist House into confusion by the arrest of its Clerk, and to delay its lawful proceedings. Their anger and excitement knew no bounds and they lost no time in making preparations for a still more reckless and revolutionary movement. It was openly asserted by Speaker Douglass and other members of the Republican House that the order for the arrest of Rich would be enforced and that he would be brought before the bar of the Republican House on the following day. With this determination several hundred Republicans gathered at the party headquarters and tendered their services to the officers of the Douglass House to aid in stopping the proceedings of the Dunsmore House. Over fifty of these volunteers were sworn in as deputy Sergeants-at-Arms and were placed under the command of R. B. Welch, of Shawnee County.

This portentious and menacing movement was met by a resolution of the Constitutional House to exclude from the hall all but members of the House. The attempted arrest of Chief Clerk Rich was deemed ample justification for the Populists in preparing to resist further outrages, and the Sergeant-at-Arms was instructed to keep out deputies and other so-called officers of the Republican House. Several Constables appeared at Representative Hall during the afternoon with warrants for Breidenthal, Ryan, Scott, Willitts and Gish, against whom complaints had been filed on account of their defense of Rich, charging them with breaking the peace. At the conclusion of the proceedings of the House they appeared before the Justices and gave bonds for their appearance.

Governor Lewelling was in consultation nearly all of Tuesday afternoon with the Populist leaders, who, appreciating the gravity of the situation and the fact that the Republicans were now committed to any folly, however desperate, urged him to call out the militia to protect the property of the state and avert bloodshed. The Governor sent for Sheriff J. M. Wilkerson, of Shawnee county, and asked him to lay aside all partisan prejudice, recognize the legal House and protect its chief clerk, Ben. Rich, and other officers. The sheriff declined to take any part in the controversy or to recognize either House. Later on, the same day, the Governor sent Sheriff Wilkerson the following formal demand:

TOPEKA, Kan., February 14, 1893.

DEAR SIR:—Whereas, a body of armed and lawless men have this day attempted to arrest the chief clerk of the House of Representatives, the Hon. Ben. C. Rich, and whereas, there are rumors, which seem to be well founded, that such lawless body of men now contemplate a second attempt to arrest said Rich and otherwise to become a menace to the peace and order of the State; now, therefore, I hereby demand of you that you proceed at once to provide such peace officers as may be necessary for the preservation of the peace and safety of the State, and that such officers be at once stationed upon the capitol grounds and in the corridors of the capitol building, as may be necessary to prevent the entering of armed or disorderly men, and that you use every lawful means in your power to preserve peace, prevent riot and all disorderly conduct, to the end that the House of Representatives may proceed undisturbed in the legitimate performance of its duty.

Please advise me at once if these demands will be complied with.

L. D LEWELLING,
Governor of Kansas.

The Sheriff also received the following from Speaker Dunsmore:

TOPEKA, KAN., Feb. 14, 1893.

J. M. Wilkerson, Sheriff of Shawnee County:

DEAR SIR:—I hereby call on you as Sheriff

of Shawnee County for sufficient force to preserve the peace and authority of the House of Representatives. I am very truly yours, J. M. DUNSMORE,
Speaker of the House of Representatives.

The Sheriff refused to comply with the demand of the Governor and Populist Speaker, and so notified them in the following communication:

TOPEKA, KAN., Feb. 14, 1893.
Hon. J. M. Dunsmore:

DEAR SIR:—Your communication calling on me as Sheriff for sufficient force to preserve the peace and authority of the House over which you preside received, and in reply will say, if there is a House of Representatives legally organized it is clothed with the power to appoint a Sergeant-at-Arms who has all the power necessary to enforce the authority with which he is invested by the House. Not wishing to decide which House is the legally organized body, I shall take no part as long as the peace and quiet of the citizens remain undisturbed.

Yours truly, J. M. WILKERSON.

Receiving no response to his demand upon Sheriff Wilkerson, Governor Lewelling late that night sent the following:

John M. Wilkerson, Sheriff of Shawnee County:

DEAR SIR—Since you have not seen fit to comply with my request to respond to a former communication of this evening, I hereby withdraw my demand for official assistance from you in preserving the peace in and about the corridors of the Capital to-morrow morning. L. D. LEWELLING,
Governor of Kansas.
Topeka, February 14, 1893.

It was on this day that the Senate concurred in the amendments to the appropriation bill passed by the House, to pay all members and employes of the Populist House their salaries, and the Douglass House becoming alarmed passed the following:

Resolved by the House of Representatives of the State of Kansas, That the treasurer of the State be and is hereby admonished not to pay any public moneys under any pretended act of the Legislature of this state passed by the body presided over by J. M. Dunsmore, and now pretending to be a House of Representatives; and be it further

Resolved, That said State Treasurer and his bondsmen will be held strictly responsible for any moneys so paid out of the public treasury, and under no circumstances or conditions whatever will this House ever ratify, confirm or otherwise make good to said Treasurer any such money so paid under said pretended authority.

This bill, which was signed by the governor during the evening, made an appropriation of $30,000 for the per diem and mileage of the members of the Senate and of the Populist House, and went into effect up on its publication in the official state paper the following morning.

In the senate H. H. Artz was confirmed as adjutant general.

THE TEMPEST BREAKS.

A REPUBLICAN MOB MARCHES UPON THE CAPITOL—HALTED BY THE GUARDS—A WILD CHARGE UP THE MAIN STAIRWAY—THE IMMORTAL SLEDGE HAMMER—THE UNLOCKED DOORS OF REPRESENTATIVE HALL BATTERED DOWN—INSURGENTS IN FULL POSSESSION—RECRUITING THE RANKS OF THE RED BADGED DEPUTIES.

The most extraordinary scenes ever witnessed in the Capitol of Kansas occurred on Wednesday, February 15, when the Republicans ceased their masquerading, battered down the doors of Representative Hall, took forcible possession of the room and barricading the approaches, inaugurated a seige that will forever be memorable in the annals of Kansas. By their action they made it necessary, the Sheriff having refused the Governor the protection he had demanded, for the Governor to call out the Militia and transform the State House grounds into an armed camp, where in the absence of other shelter from the severe winter weather the men used the corridors of the building as temporary barracks.

The night had passed without any event of especial importance transpiring. The appropriation bill signed by the governor on the previous evening was published in this morning's official state paper, and before 9 o'clock the members of the House and Senate and the officers and employes of the Dunsmore house had nearly all received their warrants from the Auditor and their money from the Treasurer. This was the very thing the Republicans were determined to prevent, if possible, and the Attorney General having declined to take any steps toward bringing the matter before the Supreme Court, a temporary restraining order was obtained from Judge Hazen, of the Shawnee county district court, to forbid the payment. Notice of this order was served on the Auditor and Treasurer by the Sheriff about 11 o'clock, and the instructions of the court were complied with without question.

But before this more exciting events had for the time being banished from the minds of Populists and Republicans alike all financial questions.

As has already been stated, the Republicans on Tuesday afternoon swore in scores of Assistant Sergeants-at-Arms and several hundred Deputy Sheriffs were subsequently swore in by Sheriff Wilkerson. There was a general feeling of apprehension. Everything portended trouble and daylight was awaited with a degree of anxiety that it is impossible to describe. The open threats of the officers of the Douglass House that they would yet arrest Ben Rich, led his friends to prevail upon him to spend the night at the Capitol, and anticipating an attack before morning from the forces under R. B. Welch, the Sergeant-at-Arms of the Dunsmore House accepted the services of a number of volunteer assistants. No attempt, was made, however, to capture Mr. Rich, who, together with his books and vouchers, had in the evening been transferred to the auditor's office to put in the night in preparations for the payments authorized by the Appropriation bill. Many of the Populist officers and members spent the night with the guards in Representative Hall, or participating in some of the numerous conferences that took place in the offices of the Governor and the Adjutant General. With the return of day all had gone home save a few of the guards, who were left with orders from Speaker Dunsmore that aside from members and reporters none but the officers and employes of the Dunsmore House should be admitted. A guard, consisting of a half dozen men, was stationed on the stairway leading to the front entrance of the hall, with instructions to direct the members of the House to use the rear entrance in order to preventy any confusion. The front doors of Representative Hall were, however, left unlocked and a few of the employes had arrived before anything out of the usual order transpired.

About 9 o'clock J. R. Miller, doorkeeper of the Republican House, appeared in the west wing of the Capitol and attempted to pass up the east stairway to the hall, when he was refused admission in accordance with the order of Speaker Dunsmore. He became enraged and evinced a determination to force his passage through the guards, but eventually thought better of it and went away, not being at all molested or interfered with, even when he used the most violent language. Miller proceeded directly to the Copeland hotel, where he found the members of the Douglass House assembled, and excitedly informed them of what had transpired. This was sufficient excuse in their minds for the resort to violence, which they had been looking forward to, and it was decided to form in line, march to Representative Hall and take possession by force. The column was headed by Speaker Douglass and Speaker pro tem Hoch, and included the members, officers and hangers on of the Douglass House to the number of about 100. As they marched toward the capitol, their number was increased until upon ascending the east steps and filing into the main corridor, the rabble had attained the proportions of a formidable mob. That they were bent on trouble was plainly to be seen from their appearance and demeanor, and from their subsequent refusal to accede to the very reasonable restrictions laid down by Speaker Dunsmore for the protection of the legal House from the confusion that had been interrupting its proceedings.

On reaching the point at which the stairway leads to the main entrance of the hall, they encountered three Populist guards, who for a moment barred their further advance. They were told quietly, but firmly that the members would be admitted at the other entrance, where they would be provided with passes, but that only members could be admitted. Speaker Douglass inquired by whose authority they were there, and they replied that it was by the authority of the Adjutant General and the Executive Council.

Douglass said, in a loud and peremptory voice: "I, as Speaker of the House, order you to get out of the way!"

The Republican phalanx then gathered themselves for the attack. A few more words passed, the assault was made, there was a momentary scuffle as the guards essayed to obey their instructions, and then with a wild yell the mob dashed forward, overcame the guards by sheer force of numbers and surged up the stairway in a mass. It was as if they were storming a fortress at whose entrance a battery was planted, and what with the crowding and shoving, the clamor and shouting of a hundred infuriated, lawless and utterly reckless men, a scene was presented that beggars description. In their eagerness to get to the top the revolutionary band almost broke down the stair rail, which would have precipitated some of their own number to certain and horrible death below.

There was no opposition to encounter at the head of the stairs, the few guards and employes who stood about having retired to the hall.

A Republican who had gone to the rear entrance and been passed into the hall as the members and newspaper men would all have been, had gone through to investigate and appearing on the landing at this juncture, shouted: "Come on, men, the way is clear!"

"Break down the doors; no quarter to the Populists!" was the cry of the insurgents as they rushed onward and took undisputed possession of the landing, though no doors were locked, nor had admission under the regular instructions been refused.

In fact, several of the members of the Douglass House, including Rosenthal, Benefiel of Montgomery, Bowers, Bowie and at least three others accepted passes the same as the Populist members, all being treated alike. Two, Sherman and Lobdell of Lane, refused passes and turned away.

Now the situation with regard to the doors of the hall was well understood by the assaulting party. It was usual during the extreme cold weather to enter the cloak room first, and toward this outer door the mob turned its attention. It was light and thin and was opened without any trouble. Once inside the cloak room, they encountered the heavy door leading into the hall, which was not locked but could have been opened by a child. This was not, however, in accordance with the Republican programme and without trying the knob Douglass and Hoch pounded on the door and demanded admission.

L. F. Dick, sergeant-at-arms of the Dunsmore House, was among those in the hall, and three different times he called out that it was unnecessary to beat the door down, as it was not locked, and they could come in.

"On behalf of the representatives of the people, I demand that this door be opened to admit the constitutional and legal House of Representatives," cried Speaker Douglass.

"Force it open!" was loudly suggested by other voices.

This had been the plan from the beginning, and a sledge hammer had been taken along for just such an emergency. This was now passed to Speaker Douglass, who lifted the hammer and struck the door a violent blow. The panels were soon crushed, the pieces falling inside the hall. Through the aperture thus made the leaders of the mob saw a group of a half dozen Populists, including Sergeant-at-Arms Dick, who was standing close to the door trying to make them understand that it was not locked. But Speaker Douglass pounded away until he was exhausted, and was relieved by Representatives Swan and Sherman of Shawnee.

In the front rank of the assaulting party, with Douglass and Hoch, was Representative Elting, of Ness, who, in the temporary lull to enable Douglass to get his second wind, trust his arm through the broken panel and presented a revolver close to Dick's breast. Representative Troutman, who, at the beginning of the scuffle at the foot of the stairway, had ducked his head, made a rush between the guards and gained the top of the stairs, had entered the hall with the Populists, and from the inside he kept calling to the insurgent party, "Come on!" "Beat it in!" etc. Sergeant-at-Arms Dick pushed him aside twice, but he could not be repressed in his efforts to incite from a safe vantage ground still further violence.

At length the unlocked door was battered to kindling wood, and through its wreck the triumphant conspirators marched in with a great shout that could be heard blocks away. In the din and tumult that followed the con-

spirators took complete possession of the
hall, and the reign of anarchy was fully established. After a period of frenzied rejoicing, congratulations and handshaking,
the rebel House was called to order and
went through the pretense of transacting
the regular business of the day.

Having obtained complete control of the
hall, the Republicans determined to hold it
at all hazards and the large force of Assistant Sergeants-at-Arms being on hand to aid
in this plan, R. B. Welch was appointed
chief of the Sergeants and instructed by
Speaker Douglass to take charge of the hall
and hold it. Welch had already 100 Assistant Sergeants who had been sworn in the
night before and in less than ten minutes
after the capture of the hall by the Republican mob they were all there and ready for
duty, while their chief continued to swear
in additional deputies throughout the forenoon until by 1 o'clock in the afternoon
the force numbered over 300 men ready to
go to any extent to defend the illegal Republican House and prevent the Constitutional House presided over by Mr. Dunsmore from resuming business. These
deputies included business men, mechanics
from the Santa Fe shops, beardless youths
from the colleges, local politicians and representatives from almost every element
from the highest to the lowest. The majority were from Topeka and were merely there
"for the fun there was in it," or the few
paltry dollars they expected to get for their
services. As each man was sworn in, a red
badge on which was printed "Assistant Sergeant-at-Arms," was pinned to the lapel of
his coat, and as the supply of these badges
seemed to be inexhaustible, it would appear
that to have so large a number printed beforehand the Republicans must have not
merely anticipated, but actually planned
eaxctly what came to pass.

THE CALL TO ARMS.

INSURGENTS ENTRENCH THEMSELVES BEHIND
STRONG BARRICADES —MORE ARRESTS OR-
DERED.—THEY MAINTAIN THEIR DEFIANT AT-
TITUDE AND GOVERNOR LEWENLING ISSUES
HIS PROCLAMATION CALLING OUT THE NA-
TIONAL GUARDS —HE IS DENOUNCED AS A
USURPER BY THE DOUGLASS HOUSE.

Chief Welch divided his force into squads
of ten each and appointed a superintendent
to the control of each ten men. Probably
half the entire number of deputies remained on the floor to instill courage in the
hearts of the revolutionists by their presence, while one detachment was placed on
guard at the west entrance of the hall and
another at the east entrance, where, it may
be added, the main doors were locked, as
they had been for several days by common
consent, to keep out the cold, of which fact
the attacking party was so well aware that
no assault at this point was ever thought of.
Guards were also placed at the foot of the
stairways and orders given to admit no one
but members of the Legislature or those
holding passes signed by Speaker Douglass.
Every officer of the Dunsmore House was
excluded from the hall.

Not satisfied with these precautions and
conscious of the fact that the outrageous
and violent seizure of the hall would call
for decisive action on the part of the legally
constituted authorities and custodians of
the building, the Republicans proceeded
forthwith to entrench themselves against an
assault that was anticipated. Heavy bolts
were placed on the inside of each door by
carpenters ordered in for that purpose; the
doors were all barricaded with massive timbers, and all the seats, desks and tables not
in use were pulled up and stacked against
the doorways as a barricade, a step ladder
being placed at one of the transoms as a
means of entrance and exit. Fire arms,
clubs and ever conceivable description of

weapons were passed around until every man and boy was armed, for they fully expected that the Governor would send the Militia to eject them. The stairway leading to the main entrance was blocked near the upper landing with more desks, benches, chairs, timbers and every article that would offer the slightest resistance. The Speaker's entrance at the west end of the hall was similarly protected, and some of the doors leading into the departments on the next floor below were nailed shut, to the great inconvenience of the officials and their clerks.

The deputies were all heavily armed, and later on several cases of rifles and ammunition were smuggled into the hall, with the plain intention of holding it against all comers. But the pretended House was left in undisturbed possession, and gradually awoke to the fact that instead of being victors the members had simply placed themselves in the position of prisoners of war. The chairs on the Populist side of the House remained vacant, and realizing that it was impossible to legislate under such circumstances, the House of Dunsmore abandoned the hall to the Douglass forces. The room occupied by Chief Clerk Rich, together with the several committee rooms conceded to the use of the Populists, was seized, and two or three clerks of the Dunsmore House were forcibly ejected from the floor. One of these was H. W. Burdick, assistant Journal Clerk of the Populist House, Assistant Sergeant at-Arms Clogston officiating with others in this outrage. The Republicans decided that, having secured possession of the hall, it was their duty to hold it, and so they remained in continuous session throughout the noon hour, the Speaker instructing the Sergeants not to leave the room. Baskets of provisions were brought from the Copeland hotel for the relief of the hungry members and the 300 officers now on the pay roll, and thus they settled down for a stay that proved to be a longer one than they anticipated.

That they gloried in their shame and regarded the outrage committed in battering down the property of the State in the light of heroism, was shown during the morning session by the presentation to Speaker Douglass of the ten-pound sledge hammer with which he broke in the doors of Representative hall. The presentation speech was made by Mr. Hale, of Rush, who eulogized the courage and pluck of the Speaker in "daring to resist anarchy and rebellion." As the sledge hammer was borne to the desk the Republican mob cheered wildly, the members rising from their seats to join in the demonstration.

MORE ARRESTS ORDERED.

Elated by their easy capture of an unprotected hall, the members of the revolutionary House, in a spirit of braggadocio, adopted a resolution introduced by Mr. Cubbison, of Wyandotte, which was as follows:

WHEREAS, The House of Representatives on Tuesday, the 14th day of February, issued its legal process for the arrest of one Ben Rich on the charge of contempt of the House; and

WHEREAS, The legally constituted officers of said House, while attempting to enforce said process, were obstructed, assaulted and interfered with by the following named persons, to wit: J. W. Breidenthal, John F. Willits, S. M. Scott, D. M. Howard, and were by said persons prevented from enforcing the order of the House; therefore be it.

Resolved, That the Sergeant-at-Arms be and he is hereby instructed to forthwith arrest J. W. Breidenthal, John F. Willits, S. M. Scott and D. M. Howard, and have them brought forthwith before this House to answer the charge of contempt of the House.

The news of the *coup d' etat* of the Republicans was soon noised abroad and reached every part of the city. It was wired out in all its minute details by newspaper correspondents and before noon it was known in every important city in the land that Kansas was in a state of open rebellion and that anarchy had planted its banners in the Hall of Representatives. The eyes of the whole Nation were turned toward Kansas, and so deep was the interest felt in the result of the people's struggle against corporation tyranny, that over 60,000 words were demanded by the eastern journals and sent out by telegraph that night.

It was in Topeka, however, that excitement rose to fever heat. Nothing to equal it had ever been exhibited since the war. From every part of the city the people hastened in the direction of the State House, until the streets east of Capitol Square were packed with eager and anxious citizens. Groups were formed and the situation was discussed from every standpoint, the Republicans being aggressive and threatening to such a degree as to add seriously to the menacing aspect of that very critical hour. It was exultingly asserted that the officers of the Kansas National Guard would ignore the orders of Governor Lewelling, *ex officio* commander-in-chief, and that the local Republican contingent had the sympathy of the sheriff to bolster up their courage. The possible consequences of a collision in which the citizens should be involved on opposing lines were considered by the more conservative element with unspeakable apprehension, and a heavy pressure was brought to bear on the Governor to exercise his constitutional authority, and call out the troops, in order to avert riot and bloodshed. The Sheriff's evident leaning toward the side of the revolutionists, seemed to make this step imperative, if the further destruction of State property was to be prevented, and peace and order were to be preserved.

Threats of personal violence to Governor Lewelling were freely indulged in, but to these he turned a deaf ear, while he calmly and deliberately counselled with his advisers, intent only upon averting a bloody conflict without the sacrifice of the people's interests and the people's cause. To do his duty firmly and fearlessly, yet without adding fuel to the flame of public excitement, was his sole object. He first issued the following executive order:

NOTICE TO VACATE ISSUED.

STATE OF KANSAS,
EXECUTIVE DEPARTMENT,
GOVERNOR'S OFFICE,

Whereas, I have been informed as Chief Executive of the State, that the Hall of Representatives has been forcibly invaded by an armed and insurrectionary body of men who have taken and now hold forcible possession of such hall whereby the Constitutional rights of the members of such House have been subverted and the public business of legislation prevented, I therefore order all persons except such members of the House of Representatives and employes thereof as are recognized as such by the Hon. J. M. Dunsmore, Speaker of such House, to be such members and employes, to at once vacate such Hall and the approaches thereto under penalty of forcible expulsion for their non-compliance with this order.

Witness my hand and the great seal of the State at Topeka, this 15th day of February, 1893.   L. D. LEWELLING,
Governor.

When it became evident that the Insur-gents proposed to maintain their hostile and defiant position, the Governor, shortly before noon, yielded to the advice of his friends and the dictates of his own judgment and issued the following

PROCLAMATION CALLING OUT THE TROOPS:

WHEREAS, In obedience to the requirements of the Constitution of the State of Kansas, both branches of the State Legislature convened at the Capitol, in the city of Topeka, on Tuesday, January 10, 1893, for the purpose of enacting proper laws and making such suitable provisions for the future as the interests of the people of the State require at their hands; and

WHEREAS, Each branch of the Legislature was duly organized, the Hon. Percy Daniels, Lieutenant Governor, being *ex-officio* President of the Senate, and that body having elected W. L. Brown as Secretary and David Shull as Sergeant-at-Arms thereof; and the House of Representatives having elected Hon. J. M. Dunsmore Speaker, Hon. R. H. Semple as Speaker *pro tempore*, Ben C. Rich as Chief Clerk and Leroy F. Dix as Sergeant-at-Arms thereof; and

WHEREAS, The Legislature being thus duly organized, each branch thereof was duly recognized by the other, and the Legislature of the State thus constituted was and ever since has been recognized by the Executive as the proper law-making power of the State; and

WHEREAS, Certain persons who were duly elected as members of the House of Representatives, together with certain other persons who also claim or allege that they were chosen as members of the Legislature, have set up and organized a pretended House of Representatives, in opposition to and in obstruction of the lawful House of Representatives, organized and recognized as aforesaid; and

WHEREAS, Said pretended House of Representatives has assumed to elect a Speaker and other officers therefor, and ever since the said 10th day of January has obstructed and is still obstructing the lawful House of Representatives in the performance of its proper duties as one branch of the Legislature of the State; and

WHEREAS, Said pretended House of Representatives and members thereof have repeatedly threatened personal violence and injury to the members of the lawful House of Representatives, and without authority of law have called to their aid certain persons pretending to be or assuming to be Sheriffs or Deputy Sheriffs, or other civil officers, in order to maintain said unlawful organization as a pretended House of Representatives; and

WHEREAS, It is the exclusive right of each House of the Legislature to determine for itself who are entitled to seats therein, or who constitute the membership thereof, and the Courts of the State have no power or jurisdiction to inquire or determine said questions; and

WHEREAS, The Hon. J. M. Dunsmore, Speaker of the House of Representatives, has officially informed the Executive of the State that the House over which he presides is menaced by the presence of a large number of persons who have obtruded themselves into the hall of the House of Representatives in a manner indicating a lawless and insurrectionary purpose to break up the lawful House of Representatives, and drive the officers thereof from their Hall, and from the Capitol building; and

WHEREAS, Said unlawful organization has unjustifiably and arbitrarily and unlawfully assumed to order the arrest of the Chief Clerk of the lawful House of Representatives, with a view of precipitating a collision betwen said unauthorized and unlawful body and the lawful House of Representatives and its officers and members, and has with force and violence broken down the doors of the Representative Hall, and forcibly ejected therefrom the officers and members of the legal House of Representatives; and

WHEREAS, In order to avert, if possible, any resort to the military arm of the State to preserve the public peace, and to enforce the laws of the State, I applied to and directed the Sheriff of the County of Shawnee, in whose jurisdiction the capital of the State is situated, to protect the said House of Representatives in its constitutional rights and to so preserve the peace as to enable said House to peaceably continue its deliberations, and said Sheriff has failed and refused to comply with said order and directions; and

WHEREAS, The public peace should be preserved, and the rights of the House of Representatives should be respected, to the end that the people of this State may be protected in all their rights: now

Therefore, Deeming the present condition of public affairs as presenting an extraordinary occasion, and as warranting the exercise of the power vested in me by the constitution of the state, to see that the laws are faithfully executed, that the public peace may be preserved, and all persons who unlawfully obstruct the House of Representatives or any members or officers thereof in the proper discharge of their duties, may be removed, and that all unlawful organizations may be suppressed and violence and bloodshed may be averted.

I, L. D. Lewelling, Governor of the State of Kansas, in virtue of the power vested in me as Commander-in-Chief, with the power to call out the militia to execute the laws and suppress insurrection, do hereby call forth the militia of the State in order to suppress said unlawful assemblage, and to restore peace and protection, and to cause the laws to be duly executed.

Adjutant General Artz is hereby charged with the duty of issuing the necessary orders to carry into effect the purposes hereinbefore declared.

I appeal to all loyal and law-abiding citizens to favor, facilitate and aid this effort to maintain the supremacy of the law, and the honor and integrity and perpetuity of the state.

In witness whereof I have hereunto set my hand and caused the great seal of the state to be affixed at the executive office in the capitol at Topeka, this 15th day of January, 1893.   L. D. LEWELLING.

By the Governor.
    R. S. OSBORN, Secretary of State.
By D. C. ZERCHER, Ass't Sec'y of State.

INDICATIONS OF MUTINY.

The office of the Adjutant General became immediately the center of interest and was beseiged by those who had counsel to offer, or who desired to volunteer their services for the maintainance of law and order, and of the integrity of the state. Short as were those winter days, a provisional company was organized before nightfall and mustered in under command of Judge McDonald, of Parsons, and a second one under command of H. C. Lindsay, of Topeka.

It has frequently been asserted, and correctly, that the first company of the Kansas National Guards to be called out, and the first to respond, was Company C, of Oakland. The facts in the case, however, place their response to the call in a somewhat different light from what has been currently reported as the correct one. The Oakland company was ordered out the night previous to the proclamation calling out the State militia, and they were instructed to report for duty at the State House at 7 o'clock the following morning (February 15). This the company failed to do, giving as their excuse that their overcoats were in the armory, though the morning was clear and bright, and had they obeyed orders they would have marched directly to the armory where their overcoats were. But they delayed their movements until the Douglass crowd had broken into the hall, and thus lost the opportunity of playing a very important part in the history of the State.

Colonel Hughes was also in the conspiracy. Being absent from the city the Governor had the Adjutant General telegraph for him. The Colonel reported that morning in a very pompous manner, informing the Governor that he was ready for duty and inquiring if he should don his uniform. On being informed that that was the proper thing to do under the circumstances, he went home for that purpose and absented himself two and one-half hours. In the meantime the Douglass mob had accomplished its object and broken down the doors of Representative Hall.

This delay on the part of the Oakland company, and on the part of Colonel Hughes, gave the Governor his first intimation that the militia could not be relied upon and he thereupon proceeded to organize provisional companies.

Orders were sent by telegraph to Co. G, of Marion, Battery A, of Wichita, and later Co. A, Third regiment, Eureka; Co. B, Third regiment, Holton; Co. A, Second regiment, Wichita; Co. F, Third regiment, Howard, and Co. C, Fourth regiment, Clyde. Bat. B, of Topeka, was ordered out. The Wichita battery was ordered to bring a Gatling gun.

Replies to these orders came in slowly, and it looked as if the Republican prediction of a general mutiny might not be wholly groundless. The spirit of defiant rebellion spread with alarming rapidity, and the apprehensions of the conservative and law-abiding element of both parties were not quieted when on the arrival of Company C from Oakland it was greeted with derisive yells from the Republicans who were massed by thousands in front of Capitol Square, where the throng was being constantly augmented by new arrivals. At 2 p. m. this company, forty strong, entered the State House and established their barracks in the large hall on the ground floor of the south wing, assuming complete charge of all the entrances, stacking arms and making themselves as comfortable as possible. State officers and Supreme Court Judges having offices in that wing were supplied with passes and military discipline prevailed everywhere.

At 3 p. m. the two provisional companies who had been supplied with arms at the arsenal marched from thence to the capital building, each being subjected to the jeering and guying of the mob, which now pressed close upon the broad steps leading to the main entrance of the east wing. Judge McDonald's company was stationed at the foot of these steps, to keep the crowd back, and this afforded an excuse for an assault that added to the bitter feeling between the partisans. One of the sentries, in his effort to keep a space open, was confronted by a fellow who resisted the order. The guard pressed the rifle across the fellow's breast, and gently pushed him off the walk. The man stepped up again, and again was pushed off. A half dozen men now sprang upon the walk, and the guard summoned others to his assistance, among them being Chaplain Todd, of the Populist House, who was one of the first volunteers in this provisional company. A hand-to-hand fight ensued, and for a few moments it was feared the riot would become general. White and colored men alike participated in the melee, closed in upon the guards, grabbed at their guns, and struck at them, eventually driving them back, when a couple of deputy sheriffs interfered and forced the rabble to desist from the attack. A little later, company C marched down the front steps, clearing them as they went, and reinstated the sentries in their former position. Every entrance and door throughout the building, except those leading to Representative hall, was then put in charge of two or more soldiers, with instructions to admit no one without a military pass.

At 6:45 p. m. Company C was reinforced by the arrival from Horton of forty members of Company B under command of Lieutenant Barker.

THE GOVERNOR DENOUNCED.

Upon the strength of Governor Lewelling's call for troops, the Douglass House adopted the following resolution, introduced by Mr. Greenlee, of Reno:

WHEREAS, Under our governmental system, both state and national, three co-ordinate branches are recognized, to-wit: the legislative, executive and judicial, each having well defined spheres of action, independent of the other, and

WHEREAS, The executive branch of our state government, by its governor, has in times of peace, and for partisan purposes, invoked the aid of the military forces of the state to coerce a co-ordinate branch of this government, to-wit: the legislature, therefore

Resolved, That we, the Representatives of the people of the State of Kansas, in session at the Hall of Representatives, in the city of Topeka, do enter our most solemn protest, and hereby denounce the executive of this State as a usurper, and as attempting to place the civil authorities of the State in subjection to the military thereof ;

Resolved, That, should the state executive succeed in his nefarious schemes, "the government of, for and by the people" will have perished in Kansas and on its ruins will be entrenched a goverament of military force, dominated by the exccutive, and the utter extinguishment of the legislative and judicial branches of our State government.

THE ULTIMATUM.

GOVERNOR LEWELLING'S PERSONAL APPEAL TO THE DOUGLASS HOUSE, AND THE PRUDENT COUNSEL OF EX-GOVERNOR OSBORNE, BEING DISREGARDED, COLONEL HUGHES IS ORDERED TO CLEAR REPRESENTATIVE HALL.—THE COL.- ONEL SURRENDERS TO THE INSURGENTS.— SHERIFF WILKERSON NOTIFIES THE GOVERNOR OF HIS INTENTIONS.

At 7:30 that evening, Governor Lewelling, accompanied by Colonel Fred P. Close, his private secretary, entered Representative Hall, where the Republican House was in session, and was escorted to the Speaker's desk by Representatives Sherman, Warner and others. Addressing the members of the House, the Governor said :

GENTLEMEN:—No man among you can deprecate the present situation which exists here to-day more than I do. There is no desire on the part of your Executive to institute any forcible proceedings here in this hall at the present time or at any other time. I earnestly entreat you, as citizens of the State of Kansas, as men of integrity and honor, as I know you are, to consider carefully and cautiously the conditions which exist and the possibilities which may arise in the future.

Under the present condition, there is only one course to be pursued. It is impossible that there should be any receding on the part of your Executive from the position held to-day, but I desire to ask you, as citizens, that you consider as carefully as you may do, if there may not be a way for an amicable solution of these difficulties.

I earnestly entreat you, as citizens, not to make it necessary for me to call upon the military arm of the government to enter and take possession of this Representative Hall.

There has been some talk about bringing the conditions which exist to a conclusion through the courts. It has been said repeatedly by men who are on your side, that as soon as bills are passed they would be brought into the courts, and thus a solution of this difficulty should be had. A bill has been passed by the House of Representatives and signed. If there is a method of solution of this difficulty in the courts, that method of solution is at hand; and I appeal to you, as citizens, whether it would not be better to rest your cause upon that basis, and rest upon that solution, rather than to continue to retain this hall. I urge you, as fellow-citizens, that you now surrender this hall to the legal authorities of the State. I would deprecate exceedingly to have the military enter this Hall of Representatives; I do not want anything of that kind, and I ask you, gentlemen, if you will not be willing to surrender this hall—or, at least, those of you who are not members of the House of Representatives?

Speaker pro tem Hoch was then recognized by the Chair, and spoke as follows:

Governor, pardon me—one word. I appreciate your coming not as Governor of this State, but as a citizen of this State, and I am sure I voice the sentiments of every man within the sound of my voice when I say there is no man on this floor who has ever desired anything else than a fair, honorable and amicable settlement of this unfortunate difficulty. I wish, however, Governor, to ask you in fairness if—pending this decision of the courts, which I trust will be reached within a few days—if it would not be fair, if any side abandons this hall, that both sides abandon it until this decision is reached. Could there be objection on either side to that state of affairs? I appeal to you as the Governor of this commonwealth, elected by the suffrages of the noblest and grandest people, in my judgment, on the face of the earth, elected to preside over the grandest State in the Union; I appeal to you as *my* Governor, in this critical crisis that has come upon us to-day, that if we surrender this hall, pending the decision of this matter in the courts, if it would not be fair that all parties surrender this hall during the pendency of this contest?

To this proposition for a compromise, the Governor replied:

I am not here, of course, to enter into any political discussion, or a discussion of these questions. I only ask this: You gentlemen have stated between yourselves, and it has come to my ears repeatedly, that only one thing was wanting, and that was that the House of Representatives should pass a bill that you might carry it into the courts. Now if that has been your wish prior to this time is there any reason why you should continue to hold this hall, when you have that opportunity before you? I ask you, gentlemen that you shall surrender this hall into *m* keeping to-night, that you vacate this ha and leave it to my care. I ask that you d that. I ask it of you as citizens, as country-men—many of you are personally known to me, many of you my own personal friends! There can be no harm come from this prop-osition. I ask, therefore, that you vacate this hall, surrender it to me, if you choose, and then let the process that you see fit to pursue, follow. That is all I have to say, gentlemen, further than to add that as the matter now stands it becomes my duty to use some method, which I almost shrink from naming, to secure possession of this hall, I trust there will be no occasion for anything of the kind.

Mr. Hoch, again addressing the Gover-nor, said:

Pardon me. The proposition that was made was not intended to disturb the policy that has been pursued here for more than five weeks. If both sides abandon this hall, wouldn't it be right that the state of affairs which has existed here for five weeks should be continued?

To this the Governor answered:

It is not for me to enter into any contest, dispute or debate. There are several militia companies here to-day, called to do what I deem it my duty to order, and which I shrink from more than I can tell. I ask you to consider the situation.

GOVERNOR OSBORN COUNSELS PEACE.

Governor Lewelling then left the chair and was succeeded by Ex-Gov. Thomas A. Osborn (Republican), who had come to the hall accompanied by a citizens' committee, which included Dr. McVicar, President of Washburn College; Hon. P. G. Neel, Presi-dent of the First National Bank, and Mr. E. Bennett. The Governor made an earnest appeal for peace, advising the Republicans to calmly surrender when the militia came. He assured them that their actions of that day would be condemned by nine-tenths of the citizens of this State, and in conclusion said:

In the early days of this State there were many troublous days and nights, but this day and night are far more serious and far more dangerous to the peace of the people than any of the days or nights when our State was threatened twenty-five or thirty years ago. The Governor has told you it will become his duty to eject you. He knows that the men now occupying this hall have come here to resist, but how far we cannot say, but I believe I express the opinion of a large number of the best people of this state when I say that rather than precipitate a war upon the people it will be best for you to yield to the armed troops of the State under the command of the governor. While I do not justify any act that has been com-mitted by the Populist authorities I beg you to not force upon these people a war which

may be more bloody than this State has ever known. This free government is too good to be thrown away. It cost too much blood and too much money. Give us peace and not war.

AN ULTIMATUM.

Governor Osborn's pacific advice was re-ceived in sullen silence, but with evident disapproval. Governor Lewelling and party quietly left the hall, when the House, after listening to several inflammatory speeches, determined to surrender only when driven out at the point of the bayonet by over-whelming numbers. A committee, consist-ing of Representatives Sherman and Bowie, was sent to deliver to Governor Lew-elling the ultimatum of the revolutionary House, the doors were again securely locked and barricaded, and the members awaited the next turn of events. The Assistant Sergeants-at-Arms were cautioned by Speaker Douglass not to admit the militia or any one else unless they were n pow erful than the force in the hall, and not to use firearms without the direct command of the chief Sergeant-at-Arms. The confer-ence had lasted about a half hour.

The Republican House was emboldened to take the stand it did by the receipt earlier in the evening of numerous telegrams from points throughout the State urging the Speaker and members to stand firm and as-suring them of the early arrival of reinforce-ments to strengthen the insurrection. D. M. Clark, of Ottawa, telegraphed that he was on the way with 300 men. Col. D. R. Anthony telegraphed that 1,000 men from Leavenworth would respond to the call, and others sent word by wire that they would reach Topeka next morning with volunteers for the revolution.

COLONEL HUGHES SURRENDERS.

After receiving the ultimatum of the Douglass House—that it would surrender only at the point of the bayonet, Governor Lewelling, realizing that all hope of effect-ing an honorable compromise was at an end, issued the following:

EXECUTIVE ORDER—NO. 3.

Colonel Hughes, Commanding, H. H. Artz, Adjutant General:

SIR:—You will first proceed to clear the corridors of all persons except troops; you will then station a small detachment in the main corridors of the east and west wings of the Capitol, after which you will proceed quietly with the remainder of your forces to Representative Hall and eject all persons not specified in Executive Order No. 2, a copy of which I hand you herewith. Having removed from the hall such persons designated, you will station a detachment in and about Representative Hall and such other detachments as may be necessary to occupy the entrances to the Capitol. In no case shall any person accompany the troops to Representative Hall.

L. D. LEWELLING, Governor.
H. H. ARTZ, Adjutant General.

At 10:30 Col. J.W. F. Hughes, commanding the full strength of the militia at that time massed in or about the State House, entered Representative hall attired in the full uniform of his rank and caused one of the sensations of a sensational week by surrendering completely to the revolutionists. He was introduced by the Speaker, and said:

I was ordered by Governor Lewelling to take command of the militia called out here to-day. I did so at once. I asked him for orders; he told me I must surround the House with my men, protect the property of the State, and remove from Representative hall all men who were not recognized by Mr. Dunsmore and himself as members of the Legislature. I told him he would have to look for some other officer. [Prolonged cheering.] I am still in command, and I am going to stay there until I am relieved. I may be relieved, but I can say to you that you need have no fear to-night. No one will attempt to molest you. If I am relieved, my regiment will go with me.

The applause that followed this speech was deafening and three tremendous cheers were given for Colonel Hughes. In the morning the Colonel was summoned to a conference with the Governor and Adjutant General and was relieved from his command.

SHERIFF WILKERSON WAKES UP.

Half an hour after Colonel Hughes left Representative hall, Sheriff Wilkerson, who was doubtless informed of what was transpiring and expected to see the Administration left powerless by the mutiny of the regiment that the Colonel had predicted would go out with him, sent the following communication to Governor Lewelling:

TOPEKA, KAN., Feb. 15, 1893.
To His Excellency, L. D. Lewelling, Governor of the State of Kansas:
SIR:—I, as Sheriff of Shawnee County, am charged with the duty of preserving the peace within the territorial limits of this County. I am advised that you have called upon the Military power of the State to preserve peace in this County. I wish to inform you that this action on your part is without my consent or concurrence and is wholly unnecessary, as I have at no time intimated to you that I am unable to preserve the peace within this County.

I now wish to inform you that I am fully able and prepared to enforce the laws and preserve peace and order, and it is my intention so to do.

Very respectfully,
J. M. WILKERSON,
Sheriff of Shawnee County, Kansas.

The defection of Colonel Hughes rendered it imperatively necessary to allow the Republicans to retain possession of the hall for the time being, and they remained in session all night. The roll of the House was called each hour, and fifty-six members responded to their names. A vote of thanks was extended to the citizens from other Kansas towns who were on their way to join the insurgents, and the balance of the night was passed in singing songs of the John Brown order, and snatching "cat naps" in any position that came handy.

THE THIRD DAY.

SUPPLIES FOR THE INSURGENTS SMUGGLED THROUGH THE LINES AND HOISTED TO THE HALL BY MEANS OF ROPES—UNCLE SAM'S MAIL CARRIERS LEND A HAND — SHERIFF WILKERSON ORGANIZES A STRONG POSSE AND INSTRUCTS THEM SECRETLY—ARRIVAL OF THE "ROBINSON RIFLES"—THE SHERIFF'S "SCHEME"—THE GOVERNOR'S "REMOVAL" SUGGESTED—CHIEF WELCH'S FRANTIC APPEAL TO THE SANTA FE FOR REINFORCEMENTS.

In the first gray dawn of morning, on February 16, 1893, the capital of the great commonwealth of Kansas presented the appearance of a city in a state of siege. True, the tattered remnant of the old flag still floated over the east wing of the State House, and a peaceful quiet prevaded everywhere, but through the mist that enveloped the massive

Capitol building like a cloud could dimly be discerned the gleam of campfires, armed sentries pacing their beats, the blue uniforms of the Kansas National Guards, and the first companies turning out for a morning drill on the paved streets. There was all the pomp and circumstance of war, and Kansas was, in fact, as was declared by many a speaker and through the columns of the newspapers at that time, on the verge of armed revolution.

Who were the revolutionists? What was the cause of this ominous situation in the most populous, powerful, wealthy and intelligent State in all the Trans-Missouri Empire? What brought this force of troops together and transformed the quiet Capital into a seat of war? Those who have carefully followed the chain of events described in the preceding chapters, have seen revealed the hypocrisy of the Republican leaders and their pretended House of Representatives, who, ostensibly seeking a peaceable solution of the legislative problem through the court, secretly acted in such a manner as to precipitate a crisis, involve the authorities in the possibility of a bloody conflict, pit friends against friends and brothers against brothers, and well nigh bring ruin as well as disgrace upon Kansas.

The Republicans had now committed two overt acts by which they hoped to bring about a serious crisis, and by the aid of a partisan judiciary and the force of overwhelming odds, overthrow the administration and maintain their supremacy in the House of Representatives. They had arrested the Chief Clerk of the legal House on a ridiculous charge, and had threatened to unseat the Populist members arbitrarily. When the latter sought to defend their rights as law-makers, their opponents had resorted to violence. Yet even now the law-abiding members of the legal House refused to become a party to the disgrace of the State by risking a collision with the Republicans, and so left the latter in undisputed possession of the hall they had seized by force, and after a quiet meeting in the Governor's parlor, adjourned until 1:30 p. m. of this day.

All night long the camp fires blazed on Capitol Square, and about these the members of the different reliefs huddled to keep themselves warm. The State House and surrounding grounds had been placed under complete military control after the incident in front of the main entrance on the evening before. The guards were advanced from the building and entrance to the front fence, where a strong line of pickets patrolled the whole square, while a cordon of sentries was thrown around the entire building at a distance of about 200 feet from it. The enclosure was thus transformed into a military camp and became forbidden ground for those who did not wear the uniform of the Kansas National Guards, or carry a pass from the proper authorities. The regulations of the preceding afternoon were made more stringent and the last link in a perfect military discipline was supplied.

Two more companies of militia arrived at 5 o'clock this morning, being Battery A, Light Artillery, from Wichita, with its Gatling gun, and Co. G, Second Regiment, Kansas National Guard, from Marion.

The night had been one of anxiety, within as well as without the State House. Governor Lewelling, Private Secretary Close and the members of the Executive Council of State, as well as a number of prominent citizens, apprehensive of the final result, remained up all night in the Governor's private office, where consultations were held hourly and every conceivable plan for settling the trouble without bloodshed was discussed. It was only after weighing the matter in his own mind for hours and taking the advice of his most trusted friends, that Governor Lewelling had decided to call out the militia, and he was determined to exhaust every pacific means for an adjustment of the legislative differences before resorting to the extreme measure of calling into requisition the military forces of the State.

Of course the Republican House could not remain in continual session for any great length of time without being supplied with food and refreshments from the outside, and as the guards were instructed to allow no one to enter without a pass, the scheme adopted at noon Wednesday became impracticable for further use. It could never have been utilized but for the presence of Republican sympathizers in the ranks of the militia, who deliberately violated their instructions to refuse admittance to all persons not provided with proper passes, in order to relieve the besieged. It is preposterous to think that passes would have been issued for such a purpose by the Governor or Adjutant General, so that the inevitable conclusion is forced upon us that the lines were passed through connivance upon the part of the guards.

A yet more gross violation of military orders and discipline was shown when, at 10 o'clock that night, the Populists discovered that provisions and coffee were being sent up to the imprisoned members and officers of the Douglass House by means of ropes lowered from the hall windows to the ground. They immediately proceeded to put stop to it, but those on the inside had already been so liberally supplied that no inconvenience was suffered until next morning. Then many of the members came out in squads and breakfasted, returning with as much as they could carry for the Deputy Sergeants-at-Arms, who did not dare to leave the hall for fear they would not be permitted to return. As there were so many of these Deputies that the demand could not be met in this manner, several of the United States mail carriers were pressed into service. New mail sacks were filled with provisions and ten-gallon cans of hot coffee, above which a few old papers were placed, and thus equipped the federal employes proceeded to relieve the insurgent garrison of Representative Hall. In order that they might not be interfered with in their illegal and unjustifiable work, the United States Marshal and his Deputies were on hand to arrest any Guard or officer who attemped to interfere with the United States mails (?) and thus the hungry Deputies were supplied with eatables and drinkables.

COLONEL HUGHES RELIEVED.

Upon the dismissal of Colonel Hughes from the command of his regiment at 9 o'clock on this morning, he was succeeded by Lieutenant Colonel George Barker, of Holton, who did not, however, succeed to the command of the entire force of militia concentrated on the State House grounds. On the contrary, the governor sent to the Senate the name of Hon. I. H. Hettinger, of Sedgwick, to be a Brigadier General of the Kansas National Guards, with the intention of making him the commandant of the troops as soon as his nomination should be confirmed.

THE SHERIFF CALLS FOR VOLUNTEERS.

At 9:30 a. m., in pursuance of a plan agreed upon the night before, Sheriff John M. Wilkerson appeared in the Copeland Hotel lobby and issued his proclamation, calling upon able-bodied men twenty one years old and upwards to enlist as Deputy Sheriffs, for the ostensible purpose of preserving the peace. Three recruiting stations were opened—one at the Copeland club room, one at the hall of Lincoln Post No. 1, Grand Army of the Republic, and the other at the Sheriff's office in the Court House. The first to respond to this call for volunteers was Col. A. B. Campbell, Adjutant General under Governor Martin's administration, who was appointed Chief Deputy and placed in command. The next was Rev. W. F. File, the well known pastor of one of the Topeka churches. By 11:30 a m. nearly 500 deputies had been sworn in, when a large detachment was sent to the Santa Fe Depot to meet and disarm the Provisional company en route to Topeka from Lawrence to assist the Governor and the militia forces. This company was formed from the ex-members of the famous Robinson Rifles, one of the oldest military organizations in the State, which was reorganized through the instrumentality of Ex-Governor Robinson himself to aid the the State authorities in suppressing the rebellion. Inasmuch as the Lawrence contingent came unarmed and was about 100 strong, it was not molested by the valiant deputies, who returned to the Copeland.

At noon the "Robinson Rifles," Capt. W. H. Sears commanding, reported to Adjutant General Artz, after which, by the instruction of the Governor, they attempted peaceably to gain admission to Representative hall. They were without uniforms, arms or any warlike paraphernalia, and were directed to forego all force or violence, but if possible to accomplish an entrance as citizens of Kansas. They were, however, summarily driven back from the door of the cloak room by the guards. There was not a blow struck, nor even a struggle. The company then marched out of the Capitol single file and equipped themselves from the Adjutant General's supplies at the arsenal.

DEPUTIES SECRETLY INSTRUCTED.

At 1 p. m. the entire force of deputy sheriffs was marched to Lincoln Post hall, where the doors were closed and guarded, all but regularly sworn officers being excluded. Here the work of organization proceeded under the direction of Col. Campbell. Thirteen companies of twenty-four men each were formed and placed under the command of an equal number of experienced officers. There was also one company consisting of forty-one men, to the command of which Captain A. M. Fuller was assigned. This was supposed to be the flower of the posse. Sheriff Wilkerson explained to the captains his plan of campaign, which was not to take the initiative, he said, in any case, but in the event of an attempt by the militia or any other force to remove the Republican House from the Hall of Representatives, he should move on the Capitol with his whole force, take possession at any cost and prevent the ejectment of the insurgents.

Colonel Campbell made an address to the entire force, advising extreme caution, after which the fourteen companies were dismissed with orders to report at once at designated points, such as the Copeland Hotel, the National Hotel, Republican headquarters, etc. Captain Fuller's company remained at Grand Army hall, but all were ordered to be held in readiness to act at a moment's notice. The work of recruiting was continued until upwards of a thousand citizens were sworn in and decorated with blue badges, printed with the words "Deputy Sheriff." But they were destined never to be called upon to act, and it was perhaps well for them that they were not. They were but indifferently armed, some having rifles, shotguns and revolvers, though more were equipped with base ball bats and ordinary clubs, with which they expected to have no difficulty in beating out the brains of the Populists and stampeding the National Guards.

It may be said right here that their plans are supposed to have been as follows: The blue-badged Deputies were to march upon the State House, where the Militia who were disposed to mutiny were expected to join them and the combined force was to invade the Capitol from the east front. At a pre-arranged signal, the red-badged Assistant Sergeants-at-Arms would leave Representative Hall and take up a position in the corridor of the west wing. The Governor, the Populist State officials and the loyal Militia and provisional troops, would thus be hemmed in between two fires and would be compelled to surrender unconditionally or be shot down in their tracks. The "removal" of the Governor had already been so openly suggested to the reckless opposers of the administration that it became necessary in order to allay public excitement and apprehension to publish the fact that his personal safety was amply provided for by his friends.

CHIEF WELCH APPEALS TO THE SANTA FE.

R. B. Welch, Chief of the Assistant Sergeants-at-Arms, continued to add to his force until its number became quite formidable. The list included bankers, merchants, lawyers, physicians, Washburn students, students of the State University and about every class that could have been drawn from. Had Chief Welch had his own way the entire Santa Fe shop strength would have been added to his army.

One of the amusing incidents of this very trying time, but a significant one for all that, was his attempt to have the shopmen ordered out. It was just after the news reached the Republican House that Governor Lewelling had called out the National Guards. Mr. Welch was greatly excited at the tidings and declared he would at once summon to the aid of the insurgents all the Santa Fe shopmen. He ran to the telephone and called up the office of Geo. R. Peck, to whom he made known his wishes in an agitated, yet peremptory manner. Mr. Peck was, however, too old to be caught in this style and the shops were not closed down on that day.

The details of this little episode were thus related in the Topeka State Journal of February 15:

When it was learned that the Populists would call out the militia, the Republicans in the House were greatly incensed. "I'll fix 'em," yelled R. B. Welch, of this city. "Where is a telephone?"

"In the Sergeant-at-Arms' room," some one replied. A rush was made for the room, and Mr. Welch and two other men broke in the door. A young man captured the telephone, but he was jerked away, and Mr. Welch called for "George R. Peck, Santa Fe offices." This caused a sensation, but a minute later the sensation was doubled. "Mr. Peck, I wish you would order out all the shopmen you can get." There was delay in receiving response to the telephone, but as soon as the object of the telephoning was learned the Republicans went wild with excitement and enthusiasm.

MR. WELCH'S STATEMENT.

The same paper, in its issue of February 18, contained a statement from Mr. Welch as to how he happened to call on the Santa Fe shopmen, which fully confirms the truth of this interesting bit of history. It was as follows:

CAMP DOUGLASS, February 18, 1893.
To the Editor of the State Journal:

DEAR SIR:—The statement in the *Journal* of a few days ago, that as commander of the Assistant Sergeants-at-Arms, I requested George R. Peck to order out their shopmen does me and those whom I represent injustice. The article was more erroneous in what it did not say than in what was said. When the door to the Sergeants-at-Arms' room containing the telephone, was broken through, your reporter, Elwood Peffer, was the first man through, and to the 'phone although he did not assist in opening the door. I do not complain of this, I rather admire the enterprise displayed as a reporter, but I gently put him to one side and called the law department of the Santa Fe. Mr. Peck was not there, and I called for Mr. Hurd, who, as I understood, talked to me, I do not know the terms I first used. I was not studying rhetoric just then. As I remember it, the conversation was a la United States. His answer was that they wished all of their employes to act as any other citizens. I replied that this was all we expected, but that I wished him to give the boys in the shops information that an assault was about to be made by the Governor's posse to disband the legal House of Representatives, and that if any of their employes wished to assist in the defense, to permit them to do so. This is all that I had thought of requesting of the Santa Fe and the reason for speaking to them was that there were more more men in a body at the shops than any other place in the state, and were near at hand. Nor do I wish to apologize for this action.

In the emergency of that time I was not disposed to consult the prejudices of either socialists or anarchists. I know many of the men working in the shops and know they have no sympathy with lawlessness and are possessed with the necessary brain, brawn and courage for the emergency. Yours truly,
R. B. WELCH.

The excuse for accepting the services of the Washburn lads is said to have been that the Republicans might thereby secure the guns with which that institution is supplied by the Federal government.

Colonel D. R. Anthony and ex-Governor George T. Anthony, Mrs. Laura M. Johns, of Salina, and Mrs. W. A. Morgan, wife of Senator Morgan, of Cottonwood Falls, were among the noted personages sworn in as Assistant Sergeants-at-arms, and decorated with red badges.

It will be seen that the warlike preparations were actively carried on, and it will readily be surmised that the citizens of Topeka who were awakened in the morning by the notes of the bugle to find thousands of strangers in the city and every incoming train swelling their number, and to see troops parading the streets and martial law prevailing on Capitol Square, had quite enough to work them up to the highest pitch of excitement. Business was practically suspended except at the hotels and restaurants, the Militia patronizing the latter and crowding their capacity, as was that of the hotels by the presence of so many unexpected guests. All day long the streets opposite the east front of the State House were thronged with people who were momentarily anticipating a collision between the opposing forces. All day long there was a line of people essaying to pass the Guards at the east gates and get closer to the scene of action. From this point the crowd filled the streets and sidewalks for a block north, east and south. Hundreds came in their vehicles and sat patiently for hours to witness the outcome of the rebellion, and the wall about the Santa Fe headquarters building was black with curious humanity. The number of women who were present was astonishing, and doubtless respect for them had not a little to with preventing an open riot, as opposing partisans now and then indulged in a heated argument that all but ended in blows. The steps of the First Baptist Church, particularly, resembled a ladies' gallery in some public hall, and the sign "Standing Room Only" might have appropriately been hung up at that point at almost any hour.

The small boy was omnipresent, and the tougher element became more boisterous and unendurable than ever. A sublime disregard of peaceful persons and pursuits was evinced, and the youth who didn't carry a club as large as himself, and talk in the tones of a Mississippi river fog horn wasn't in it. In short, the demoralizing effect of the insurrection permeated all ranks and classes, and at this remote day it seems little short of miraculous that there was not a bloody battle on the streets precipitated by some of the outrageous things perpetrated by the young and thoughtless.

A few Populists and many Republicans hastened to the city from every portion of the State to uphold the administration in its battle against disloyalty and treason, and almost every hour witnessed the arrival of fresh troops on the scene. At nightfall the Kansas National Guards concentrated at the Capital included the following:

Battery A, Light Artillery, with Gatling gun, Wichita, Capt. William Metcalf.

Battery B, Light Artillery, Topeka, Capt. W. H. Parker.

Company C, Oakland, Capt. Frank Shapter.

Company B, Holton, Capt. J. S. Jacobs.

Company G, Emporia, Captain Lewis.

Independent Rifles, Lawrence, Capt. W. H. Sears.

Provisional Company A (volunteers), Capt. J. F. McDonald.

Provisional Company B (volunteers), Captain Lindsay.

Three additional companies had also been ordere to report at Topeka—from Howard, El Dorado and Eureka.

Telegrams from Cities and Towns all over the State announced the departure of hundreds of non-combatants for the seat of war, who were about equally divided as to the side on which they were ready to serve. The situation became more critical every hour.

A TRUCE AGREED TO.

THE GOVERNOR'S PROPOSITION TO THE DOUGLASS HOUSE—A COUNTER PROPOSITION—THE GUNN HABEAS CORPUS CASE—SPEAKER DUNSMORE ON THE SITUATION—SHERIFF WILKERSON ASKS THE GOVERNOR TO SURRENDER THE CONTROL OF THE CAPITOL TO HIM—ANOTHER ALL NIGHT SEIGE AND A STORM.

During the forenoon measures were taken to bring about a peace conference, the principal promoters being ex-Governor Robinson, ex-Governor Osborne, and Colonel Lynde, of Miami. Governor Lewelling, still pursuing the conservative and prudent policy which marked his course throughout this troublous week, readily co-operated and before noon gave audience to a peace committee from the Douglass House at the Executive office. The result was that at 2 p, m., the following proposition from the Governor was submitted to the Douglass House for its acceptance or rejection, through the hands of Private Sectreary Close:

THE GOVERNOR'S PROPOSITION.

TOPEKA, Feb. 16, 1893.

The Governor offers, in the interest of peace and harmony, that he will withdraw the State militia, and not allow the Republican House or its employes to be interfered with by the Populists.

Provided, That all proceedings that have been commenced by the Republicans arising from the arrest of Ben C. Rich be dropped, and that the Populist members and employes be not disturbed by the arrest of officials or otherwise, and the Sheriff of Shawnee County discharge his deputies and does not interfere, nor try to interfere, with the acts of the Populists and State officials, including militia, and this agreement to continue in force until the close of the present session of the Legislature.

L. D. LEWELLING, Governor.

Secretary Close said: "The Governor thought that this proposition was a fair one, and in presenting it I hope you can arrange matters satisfactorily to all. There is great danger of a conflict this afternoon, and I do not believe you want to urge this upon us,

For the sake of harmony we offer this. I hope you will accept it at once. If you do not I fear that in the next hour blood will be shed."

Mr. Seaton said: "I had been asked by the Governor to present this matter. I had good reason to decline, as I knew you would not receive it."

At 2:10 the House went into executive session to consider the Governor's proposition and formulate a reply.

Mr. Sherman, of Shawnee, moved that the proposition be referred to a committee with instructions to prepare a counter proposition to be offered on the part of the Republican House to the Governor.

Mr. Swan, of Shawnee, was opposed to temporizing. "Calmly and coolly we stand here upon a vantage ground," he said, "which has been gained by hard work and skill, and we should not yield one inch."

Mr. Benefiel, of Montgomery, said this was the legal House and he was not in favor of receding in the least.

Mr. Richter, of Morris, was opposed to dealing with the Governor until he had removed the militia; this House had not, he said, menaced the Governor, nor any of his pets.

Mr. Ballinger, of Coffey, was in favor of making one more proposition to the Governor, and Mr. Eastman, of Lyon, and Mr. Cubbison, of Wyandotte, coincided with him, the latter holding that it was right to listen to any proposition looking to a settlement, although they were as determined as ever to adhere to their position.

Speaker Douglass, as a member merely, counseled the House to submit another proposition to the Governor, and Speaker Pro Tem Hoch expressed the same view, adding that the proposition would be so fair that no fair-minded man in Kansas would object to it. This idea was favored by Mr. Greenlee, of Reno; Mr. Warner, of Cherokee, and others.

The Speaker finally appointed Hoch, of Marion; Sherman, of Shawnee; Cubbison, of Wyandotte; Atherton, of Russell, and Benefiel, of Montgomery, as a committee to prepare and submit a counter proposition.

A COUNTER PROPOSITION.

At the end of half an hour the committee reported through Chairman Sherman; and after some further discussion and amendment the following was agreed upon as the counter proposition:

The House of Representatives over which Hon George L. Douglass presides, having commenced contempt proceedings against certain persons for the sole purpose of carrying the difficulties existing between it and the body presided over by Hon. J. M. Dunsmore before the courts for legal settlement, now, in the interest of peace, agrees to the following:

First.—To dismiss all contempt proceedings heretofore commenced.

Second.—The body presided over by Hon. J. M. Dunsmore to arrest Frank L. Brown, Chief Clerk of this House, and the body presided over by Hon. George L. Douglass to arrest Ben C. Rich, Chief Clerk of the body presided over by Hon. J. M. Dunsmore, both of said arrests to be upon the charge of contempt and to be made immediately, and the respective parties to apply to the Supreme Court for release by *habeas corpus*, both of said cases to be prosecuted upon the sole question of the legality of the respective Houses.

Third.—The Governor to discharge and dismiss the State militia and provisional guards.

Fourth.—The Sheriff of Shawnee County to dismiss all special Deputy Sheriffs

Fifth.—The House of Representatives presided over by Hon. George L. Douglass to have exclusive, free and undisputed possession of Representative Hall, with all appurtenances, rooms and approaches.

Sixth.—This agreement to remain in force until the Supreme Court shall have decided the issue in controversy.

Seventh.—In order to avoid misunderstanding in the future, that the agreement of these resolutions or plan of action shall be ratified by the signatures of each of the presiding officers of both contending bodies and the Governor.

Messrs. Sherman, Chambers (democrat), Benefiel, Cubbison and Atherton were appointed a committee to submit this counter proposition to the Governor, which they did immediately, returning shortly with the announcement that the Governor had asked until Friday morning at 9 o'clock to consider the proposition, at which time a conference between the Governor, the Populists and the Republicans would be held.

THE GUNN CASE.

The case of L. C. Gunn, above referred to, and which was destined to play an important part in the legislative muddle, will be spoken of more at length in another chapter. He had been arrested at his home in Labette county, on Wednesday, February 15, by C. C. Clevenger, Sergeant-at-Arms of the Douglass House, and brought to Topeka to answer to the charge of contempt in refusing to obey a summons issued by the House Elections Committee. On his arrival here, Mr. Gunn at once petitioned the Supreme Court for a writ of *habeas corpus,* which was granted, and he was released under a $500 bond, to appear at 10 a. m. on Friday, February 17, for a final hearing. The grounds on which the writ was applied for were that the Republican House was an illegal body, and had no authority to command his appearance. As a matter of fact, his offense and arrest were pre-arranged by the Republicans, in order to get the whole matter before the Supreme Court, where they anticipated a favorable decision on the legal status of the House.

SPEAKER DUNSMORE'S STATEMENT.

On the afternoon of this same day (Thursday, February 16,) the Populist House, being deprived of the use of their hall, which was in the possession of the Republicans, secured temporary quarters in the Stormont building, where it met in the afternoon at 3 o'clock and proceeded with the business of the session. Several bills were received from the Senate and read by title and it was determined to pass all important measures and adjourn at the earliest possible date. Speaker Dunsmore furnished the following statement concerning the House situation for publication:

With the attempt of the Douglass organization to arrest Chief Clerk Ben Rich, it became my duty to protect him in my office. Any other course would have been cowardly, and a recognition of Douglass and his Republican House, calculated to destroy the organization recognized by the Governor and Senate.

The claim made by the Republicans in that they took that method to get into the Courts is false. It was unnecessary to do so, for the reason that bills passed by the Legislature, as now organized, gave them ample opportunity to test any legal questions involved.

The real object of the Republicans was and is to destroy the organization over which I preside, and its records, and thus force the governor and senate to recognize them, and with the further intention of holding another election. I took such course as I deemed best to protect the House organization, instructing my sergeant-at-arms to use no more force than necessary, and in no case take life, except in defense of their persons. When my guards were over-powered I laid the matter before the governor, and he acted promptly.

I had, a short time previously, in anticipation of trouble, made a written request for such force as the Governor may believe proper under the circumstances. The question as it now stands is simply whether or not the Republican party can compel the Governor and Senate to recognize a body of men whose organization was not effected by men who were elected by the people.

J. M. DUNSMORE, Speaker.

THE SHERIFF'S IMPERTINENT DEMAND.

About 5 p. m. Sheriff Wilkerson, who had been engaged all day in organizing his posse of nearly one thousand deputies, called on Governor Lewelling and stated that he was amply prepared to defend the state property, and asked that he be given control of the capitol.

The Governor met this act of unparalleled impertinence and audacity with a prompt refusal to withdraw the militia, as he had the authority to call them out and to preserve the peace, which the Sheriff had refused to do when called upon Tuesday evening.

The Governor and the Sheriff came to no new understanding regarding the hostilities, but it was agreed that no aggressive move should be made on either side and that everything should remain in statu quo unti 9 a. m. Friday. The Sentries and the Picket lines were therefore retained about the Capitol all night, while a force of Deputy Sheriffs was detailed to patrol the grounds on the outside of the military cordon and a company of Deputy Sheriffs was held under arms at the Court House all night to be ready in case of an emergency.

A ROUGH NIGHT.

The Republican House again spent the night in Representative hall, once or twice communicating with the Governor in regard to his decision on the counter proposition. The utmost vigilance was observed to prevent an attempt on the part of the Populists to capture the hall, which was an insult to the Governor, in that it questioned his good faith in agreeing to a cessation of hostilities until 9 o'clock next morning. Speaker *pro tem* Hoch invited the company of National Guards from Marion to camp in the hall for the night, which invitation was accepted.

Captain Shafter, now ranking next to Lieutenant Colonel Barker, had command of the night force, consisting of seventy-six men. There were three reliefs, two hours on and four hours off. He had in all under arms 250 men. The boys got their first touch of rough weather this night, as a heavy snow storm set in about 9 o'clock, and continued until morning. The call of the sentries alone broke the silence on Capitol Square that night.

PEACE DECLARED.

GOVERNOR LEWELLING'S PROPOSITION ACCEPTED BY THE DOUGLASS HOUSE—THE MILITIA RELIEVED FROM DUTY AND THE SHERIFF'S POSSE DISBANDED—THE POSITION OF THE DUAL HOUSE NOT AFFECTED BY THE WAR—THE GOVERNOR SUMS UP THE RESULTS OF THE INSURRECTION.

It is settled. No blood: no victory. But there is peace.

The overtures made by Governor Lewelling for an amicable settlement of differences between the contending parties, such as would relieve the strained situation that had existed for three days, were on Friday, February 17, rewarded with success. Terms of peace were agreed upon and signed by Governor Lewelling and the committee acting for the Republican House, which agreement was, however, submitted to and ratified by a caucus of twenty or more Senators before it became binding upon the Governor, and the rebellion came to an end, with the extension of general amnesty to the insurgents rank and file. To whom belongs the credit for averting a bloody conflict and a prolonged struggle between armed forces that would have found friends arrayed against each other, neighbors against neighbors, brothers against brothers? Let the Capital, which all along so bitterly maligned and so shamefully misrepresented the Chief Executive of the State, speak, and stand convicted out of its own mouth. In its issue of February 18, it says:

"At 1 o'clock yesterday (Friday) morning there was presented to the legal House a proposition which finally resulted in a declaration of peace. It came from Governor Lewelling."

The proposition referred to called forth a lively discussion, which lasted until almost the dawn of morning, when the Republican House decided that the Governor's terms of peace were satisfactory. A committee was immediately named to announce to the Governor the acceptance of his proposition and to ratify on the part of the House the terms of the agreement. This committee consisted of Speaker Douglass, D. W. Eastman, of Lyon County, and J. K. Cubbison, of Wyandotte County. It was expected that they would be able to report to the House early in the morning, and that hostilities would cease immediately. The majority of the members, therefore, left the hall to procure the first warm meal they had enjoyed for two days, but the 300 or more deputies remained prisoners, strict orders having been given by Adjutant General Artz to the guards to admit no Assistant Sergeants-at-Arms without his authority, which it was too early to obtain.

During the night the snow had fallen steadily and the earth was covered with a white mantle ten inches in thickness. It had driven in the pickets and smothered the camp fires, from whose smouldering embers thin columns of blue smoke rose high in the clear, crisp atmosphere. The sun rose in an azure sky and poured a flood of glory over the scene. Everything breathed peace, and the load of anxiety that had for days weighed heavily on the citizens of the whole commonwealth was lifted and passed away.

BLOODSHED NARROWLY AVERTED.

The only unfortunate occurrence of the morning was brought about in the attempt to smuggle food into the state house to feed for the sixth time since their self-imposed incarceration the small army of assistant sergeants-at-arms. The deputy sheriffs had, as usual, massed themselves at their headquarters, the Copeland hotel, which was also the source from which the insurgents drew their rations. It was not deemed prudent to again resort to federal mail carriers to send provisions to Welch's forces, so about sixty of these deputies undertook to run the gauntlet with baskets of provisions and cans of hot coffee. At 9:30 they made a successful rush on the guard in front of the state house, followed closely by some twenty members of the Douglass House. In this way they broke through the lines at the gates and advanced upon the sentries, who refused to admit them to the building. The sheriffs thereupon formed a solid phalanx, charged upon the guard and went on up to the hall, hooting and yelling like a band of Apache Indians. At the moment in which the sheriffs broke through the guard lines, one of the guards snapped his Winchester, but for some unaccountable reason the weapon missed fire, and thus, in a manner which seems miraculous, bloodshed was averted. Had the Winchester been discharged there is no doubt but the most serious consequences would have followed. The cartridge which was thus snapped is now in the State Historical Society's rooms, and plainly shows the indentations made by the gun lock.

In the melee, Dr. Patee, who was acting as Assistant Adjutant in charge of the squad on duty at the entrance, was struck on the head with a club and afterwards with the butt of a revolver and was quite seriously bruised. A gash was cut in the top of his head by the revolver that bled profusely. He followed the mob up to the House and searched for his assailant but could not find him. After this breach a strong force was placed at the gates, where, owing to the truce of the preceding night but a small squad had been stationed.

A QUIET MORNING.

The deep snow, which, under the influence of a bright sun, began to melt and change the gutters into running streams, prevented the assembling this morning of a great crowd such as had occupied the streets in front of the Capitol on Thursday, and with the storm and the pacific news from the Legislative Halls all interest in, as well as all anxiety regarding the situation seemed to have been obliterated so far as the general public was concerned.

The members of the Douglass House were disappointed in their anticipations of an immediate report from the committee appointed to close the peace compact with the Governor, as there were so many minor details wanting to complete the arrangement that it was nearly noon before the document was in a shape that proved satisfactory to both sides. In the meantime two or three additional companies of militia that had been ordered to the Capitol when the situation appeared to be so critical on Thursday afternoon, put in an appearance and the State House and grounds remained in complete possession of the military authorities, no one being admitted without a pass signed by the Governor or the Adjutant General.

A block away and confronting the east entrance of the State House, Sheriff Wilkerson's army of deputies was held in readiness, upon the slightest excuse, to attempt the capture of the Capitol at a moment's notice.

No attempt was made in the Republican House to do business, but speeches were made by ex-Governor Anthony, Col. John M. Brown, Mrs. Laura M. Johns and others. Speaker Pro Tem. Hoch held the chair throughout the morning session.

THE COMMITTEE REPORT ACCEPTED.

At 12:25 p. m. the committee which had been closeted with the governor for several hours entered the hall, and its chairman, Speaker Douglass, presented to the House the agreement entered into between the committee and the Governor, which was as follows:

TOPEKA, February 17, 1893.

First—It being the understanding that the House presided over by Hon. J. M. Dunsmore has secured a hall in which to meet, the House presided over by Hon. G. L. Douglass shall remain in possession of Representative Hall undisturbed and unmolested.

Second—The House presided over by Mr. Dunsmore shall in like manner be undisturbed and unmolested in the possession of the hall which it has secured, and if it desires select a room in the State House for its meetings other than Representative Hall.

Third—No arrests to be made by either House of the members or officers of the other.

Fourth—The militia to be immediately relieved, including the new recruits sworn in, and the Sheriff's posse to be immediately disbanded.

Fifth—The militia companies now en route for Topeka to be immediately telegraphed

to by the Governor to return to their homes.
[Signed.]   L. D. LEWELLING,
                          Governor.
              GEO. L. DOUGLASS,
              D. W. EASTMAN,
              J. K CUBBISON,
Committee on the part of the House presided over by Mr. Douglass.

The following additional memorandum was attached to the agreement:

The memoranda this day signed by Governor Lewelling and George L. Douglass, D. W. Eastman and J. K. Cubbison as a committee of the House of Representatives presided over by Mr. Douglass and hereto attached, is not to be construed as a recognition by either the Douglass or Dunsmore House of the legal organization or character of the other, or by the Governor or the Senate as a recognition of either of such Houses, and shall not be used in court or in any legislative body as evidence for any person, party or body, and shall not be entered upon the journal or other record of either the Douglass or Dunsmore House or the Senate.
(Signed)   L D. LEWELLING, Governor.
              G. L. DOUGLASS,
              D. M. EASTMAN,
              J. K. CUBBISON, Committee.

The agreement was accepted by a vote of the House and a little later flags were raised upon the west wing and the dome, the stars and stripes indicating the surrender of the insurgents and their renewal of allegiance to the State and Federal Government.

THE BARRICADES TORN DOWN.

Steps were immediately taken to release the officers and members from their long confinement in Representative Hall, and on motion of Colonel Warner, Chairman of the "Barricade Committee," the work of removing the heavy timbers and other obstructions from the doors and stairways was begun and completed in the course of a couple of hours.

The continued animosity felt by some of the Republican patriots (?) toward the administration was shown by the motion made by Mr. Seaton that the decorations of the Hall, which had remained there since the inauguration of Governor Lewelling, be removed. Wiser heads saw the folly of such boys' play and there were cries of "No!" "No!" from several members, whereupon Mr. Seaton withdrew his motion. An overzealous Assistant Sergeant-at-Arms attempted to carry out the object of Mr. Seaton's motion without the authority of the House, when Speaker Pro Tem Hoch

promptly "squelched" him by threatening to order the arrest of any one removing the decorations of the Hall.

The Speaker summoned the Assistant Sergeants-at-Arms before the House later on and complimented them on their splendid(?) service for the State. "The cause of good government and law and order will always be indebted to you," he said, "as few men have ever rendered greater services to the State than you have."

In the absence of proof of other valorous deeds, it is to be presumed the heroic service of the deputies consisted in demolishing over $1,400 worth of sandwiches and coffee behind the barricades, for which the State subsequently had to pay, as well as for the aforesaid services at the rate of $3 per day.

Speaker Douglass was followed in a similar strain by Chief Deputy Welch and Speaker Pro Tem Hoch, after which three cheers were given for Commander Welch. A force of thirty Assistant Sergeants-at-Arms was appointed to remain on guard in the hall over night and about 3 p. m. the House took a recess until 10 a. m. Saturday, with the understanding that it would then adjourn until 4 p. m. Monday.

DISBANDING THE FORCES.

In the meantime the military guard around the State House had been removed, and the Adjutant General and his staff were busy issuing orders and relieving from duty the several companies of the Kansas National Guards that had been concentrated at the Capital. Telegrams were sent out countermanding the call for additional troops, and the provisional guards were relieved from duty and disbanded. Transportation was hurriedly secured for those companies anxious to leave for home on the afternoon trains, and a general order was issued by the Governor releasing all companies from service until further orders.

Sheriff Wilkerson's army was also mustered out of service during the afternoon, the battle flags were furled and the sun went down on a city and State where peace had resumed its reign after a bloodless revolution.

Of course the events of the three days of anxiety and trouble, and their final result, had no effect on the legislative muddle, but left the lower house still divided as before.

THE RESULTS OF THE WAR.

Governor Lewelling very ably summed up the results of the war in the following statement dictated on this day for the press:

The Populist party has taken no step *backward*. To the Republican House has been conceded the possession of Representative hall in the Capitol building. This does not constitute a legislative body, nor does it empower anybody to make laws that shall be recognized by the people. The concession of the hall to the Republican House is not an admission on the part of the Populists or myself that the Republican is the constitutional House. In the interests of peace and for the welfare of the people, the Douglass House has been given the use of Representative hall. Had possession of it been steadfastly claimed by the Populists, and striven for, the problem would have resolved itself for solution into a shameful physical contest. The Populist Legislature may now go on unmolested in the transaction of its business and proceed in a regular and lawful manner to the conservation of the public weal. The Governor and the Senate of Kansas will recognize but one House of Representatives.

If, at some later day, the Supreme Court shall declare the Populist House an unconstitutional body, then the responsibility for the action of the Court will rest with it alone. The people are the judges of the action of their Representatives and if there is any blame it will be cast in the right direction. It must not be lost sight of, that the Populists have at all times denied the right of the Supreme Court to determine questions pertaining to the organization of the House of Representatives.

The attempted arrest of Chief Clerk Ben C. Rich, of the Populist House, by the Republicans, and the menacing attitude of the lawless element, strengthened by Republican sanction, made the situation grave in the extreme. Had the Republicans declared the seats of the Populist Representatives vacant, as they publicly announced they would do, and attempted to arrest the members of the Dunsmore House because they persisted in remaining in Representative Hall attending to the business that the well-being of the people demanded, matters would have been brought to a crisis. In the endeavor of the Douglass House to force their illegal claims, it was zealously supported by an armed mob under the command of the Sheriff of Shawnee County, who has always been hostile to the Populist party, and it seemed certain that there would have been a bloody conflict. This condition of things seemed to make it necessary that the restraining influence of the military should be invoked. This was done, and the result to-day is that the Populist House is suffered to proceed without fear of molestation to the transaction of business. Bloodshed has been averted. This is the crowning triumph of the Populist victory.

The Populist House met on this day, and after transacting considerable business of a routine nature, adjourned to Monday, February 20, at 3:30 p. m.

BAD FAITH.

MEMBERS OF THE POPULIST HOUSE SERVED WITH NOTICE TO APPEAR IN THE DOUGLASS HOUSE OR THEIR SEATS WILL BE VACATED— THE GUNN CASE CONTINUED BY THE SUPREME COURT—THE POPULIST BODY MEMORIALIZED BY THE EXECUTIVE COUNCIL TO COMPLETE ALL NEEDFUL LEGISLATION BEFORE ADJOURNMENT.

On the day following the signing of the peace protocol, the withdrawal of the military control over the State House and grounds and the disbandment of the Sheriff's posse, there were several events of more than passing importance. Of chief interest, as it evidenced bad faith on the part of the Douglass House, was the act of the Sergeant-at-Arms, under instructions, of course, in serving notice upon the Populist members that unless they appeared before the Republican House not later than Tuesday, February 21, or showed satisfactory cause for not doing so, their seats would be declared vacant, and the Governor would be asked to call a special election in each of the fifty-six districts to fill the vacancies. This mendacious attempt at intimidation was either denounced or wholly ignored by the members of the Dunsmore House, who knew the Republicans would not dare to put the order into effect until after a decision of the Supreme Court. It was made in accordance with the resolution introduced by Mr. Seaton and adopted a few days before.

JUDGE HAZEN ENJOINS THE STATE TREASURER.

In the District Court of Shawnee County, at 9 a. m., Judge Hazen rendered his decision in the injunction case commenced by B. M. Curtis, County Attorney, against W.

H. Biddle, State Treasurer, and Van B. Prather, State Auditor, to prevent the paying out of money under authority of the appropriation bill passed by the Populist House and Senate and signed by the Governor, granting a temporary restraining order. The decision was orally delivered and very lengthy, reviewing the facts inicent to the organization of the dual House of Representatives from a Republican standpoint. The Court held that it possessed the right and power to inquire into the manner in which a House of Representatives is organized, which was the chief point raised by the attorney for the defense. It further held that this was necessary in order to prevent two or more Houses of Representatives being created under a like pretense, the two Houses now claiming to be legally organized being cited as an illustration.

On the other hand, however, the court decided that it was not vested with the right or power of inquiring into the methods by which members were elected to the Legislature, but must be guided by the credentials they held as members. The court decided that the J. M. Dunsmore House of Representatives, not having been legally organized, was not a legal House of Representatives, and ordered that the State Treasurer be and hereby is restrained from paying out monies provided for in the salary bill acted on by the Dunsmore House.

AN UNREASONABLE DECISION.

This decision has been severely criticised by the most competent legal authority in the State, and was, at the time, very generally conceded to have been based upon party expediency rather than upon law. For instance, the court admits that it has no right to inquire into the methods by which members were elected to the Legislature, but was guided by the credentials or certificates which they held as members. Yet the Republican House had already seated Mr. Rosenthal without a certificate, and, therefore, upon this decision, he was clearly not entitled to sit as a member.

Again, at the opening of the case, the Attorney General filed a motion that it be dismissed, citing a statutory provision empowering the Attorney General to either prosecute, defend or dismiss such cases. He made, in addition, the strong point that

should the case now instituted in Shawnee county, wherein the county attorney brings an action in order to establish the illegality of a certain House of Representatives, result in the Attorney General being forced to try the same, a hundred other county attorneys in the State might do likewise and demand his time to establish some other House of Representatives, or accomplish some other purpose. The motion being overruled, the Attorney General gave notice of appeal to the Supreme Court.

It was admitted by counsel for respondents that a court might, in proper cases, determine whether a "Legislature" (meaning the House and Senate considered together) which passed a Legislative enactment was a legal body, or legally in session. Such cases might arise where the journals of the two Houses show that the Legislature had voluntarily convened at a time not authorized by the constitution, and not duly called into extraordinary session by proclamation of the governor, and not reconvened in an adjourned session pursuant to its own prior adjournment legally made. But it was contended that when the two Houses of the Legislature met at the time, and at the place required by the Constitution, and proceed to organize, each having a membership equal to or greater than a majority of all the members elect thereto, and these facts appear upon the journal, and the constitution declares "each House shall keep and publish," then all questions in regard to the validity of the Legislature are foreclosed.

Further, that if there be two bodies of men, each claiming to be the House of Representatives, the co-ordinate branch of the Legislature and the Executive, in whom is vested a part of the legislative power and authority, must, for the purpose of co-operative action in the process of law making, determine which of the two is the legal House; and when they have decided that question, *it is settled, and forever.*

But these and other like powerful arguments were presented to the court in vain, and the restraining order was issued, as already stated.

THE GUNN CASE CONTINUED.

The Supreme Court convened at 10 a. m. to take up the matter of the application of L. O. Gunn for a writ of *habeas corpus.* Chief

Justice Horton presided, and there was a full bench Hon. Eugene Hagan appeared for the petitioner, and was assisted by Judge Doster, G. C. Clemens and Judge W. C. Webb, who were delegated by the Governor so to do. The State was represented by Attorney General Little. Chester I. Long, T. F. Garver and W. H. Rossington appeared for the Republicans. Counsel for the petitioner asked for a continuance, and the court, being of the opinion that all sides should be fully prepared to try so important a case, ordered the hearing continued until Tuesday morning at 9 o'clock.

THE DOUGLASS HOUSE ADJOURNS.

The Douglass House held a short session in the morning and then adjourned to 4 p. m., Monday. Several Populist members came and removed their books and private papers from their desks, where they had been left before the capture of the Hall by the Republicans. A few bills of minor importance were introduced. The floor and galleries were crowded with visitors who came out of curiosity to see how badly the Hall had been damaged during the assault and subsequent siege. Many of the wives and other relatives of the members occupied the seats of Legislators alongside their husbands or brothers who belonged to the House of Douglass, and a few officers and soldiers of the National Guard, in full uniform, were scattered among the various groups upon the floor.

THE DUNSMORE HOUSE MEMORIALIZED.

The Populist House, now that it was free to work in harmony with the Senate, had decided to enact all needed legislation as soon as possible and then adjourn sine die. This intention having been given publicity through the press, the Executive Council met and addressed the following memorial to J. M. Dunsmore, Speaker, which was signed by all the members of the Council:

It is the unanimous desire of the Council now in session that the House do not adjourn until it has passed all the important legislation demanded by the people.

A WEEK OF SUSPENSE.

PUBLIC INTEREST CENTERED IN THE GUNN HABEAS CORPUS CASE—THE REPUBLICANS THREATEN TO ESTABLISH A PROVISIONAL GOVERNMENT—A SENSATIONAL SCHEME - THE "MAXIMUM FREIGHT" BILL AND THE "AUSTRALIAN BALLOT" BILL PASSED BY THE DUNSMORE HOUSE—THE SITUATION STATED IN PLAIN TERMS.

On the following Monday (February 20) the rival Houses resumed business as if nothing had happened, the Douglass House holding its sessions in Representative Hall, while the Populists met in the improvised hall in the basement of the south wing of the State House. It was generally felt that everything now depended on the decision of the Supreme Court in the Gunn case, and owing to this element of uncertainty neither House remained in session over two hours.

R. B. Welch, who was commander of the 600 or more assistant sergeants-at-arms during "the war," was relieved from duty by the Republican House, with a set of complimentary resolutions and both this House and the Senate was visited by a delegation of eight Senators from the territory of Oklahoma.

The Republicans in caucus the same evening decided to carry out the scheme embodied in the Seaton resolution adopted a week previously, and on Tuesday declare the seats of the 54 Populist members vacant.

THE DUNSMORE HOUSE

Assembled in its new hall at 4 p. m., and was called to order by Speaker *pro tem* Semple. A large number of bills were introduced and many Senate bills passed to second reading, after which a recess was taken until 9 a. m. Tuesday.

The Senate was busily occupied with routine business and made excellent progress.

A DESPERATE SCHEME TALKED OF.

A sensation was created by the announcement on authority that would ordinarily be considered reliable, that the Republicans had arranged for about 40,000 men who could be concentrated at the Capital on twelve hours notice in the event that they should see fit to renew hostilities. It was further stated that the Republicans had perfected plans for a provisional government, if necessarry, to carry their point. This would give them the power to name election officers and place in their hands once more all the machinery of state.

A GHASTLY WARNING.

A rather sensational episode was the discovery in the passageway leading through the rotunda, of a valise filled with human bones, set close to one of the massive stone walls. The cross bones, with the lower jaw bone forming the loop at their intersection, were lashed together in the form of a cross and hung on the door leading to the north wing. Above this ghastly signal was drawn a circle, within which was a hand pointing to the sentence: "This man ventured too far. Observe his fate! Sabe?" This was all done in chalk. While a few affected to regard the matter in the light of a joke, there were many who viewed it otherwise and considered that it was a warning meant to be heeded.

This latter theory was apparently confirmed by the fact that, during the preceding week or ten days, Governor Lewelling received numerous threatening letters, which were invariably decorated by rude cuts of the ancient piratical emblem—the skull and cross-bones—aptly appropriated by the political pirates who had been plundering the state for so many years.

Tuesday, February 21.

On Tuesday morning, February 21, the hearing of the Gunn *habeas corpus* case commenced in the Supreme Court, where it continued to occupy the whole of the time until Thursday, on which day argument of counsel was heard, which enced in the matter being taken under advisement, the decision not being announced until Saturday.

In the Douglass House, Representative Seaton, of Atchison, the originator of the scheme to oust the populist members, and declare their seats vacant, moved that the resolution regarding the vacating of seats of members elect be made the special order for 11 o'clock Friday, which was in order to await the decision of the Supreme Court in the Gunn matter.

A VISIONARY SCHEME.

The Republicans held a caucus this evening to discuss the Senatorial situation, and the practicability of electing a straight-out Democrat ("Stalwart") to contest Judge John Martin's seat in the United States Senate. Hon. Bailey P. Waggener's name was presented by two of the three Democratic Representatives who acted with the Republican House—Thomas G. Chambers and Stephen Meagher—as their choice for United States Senator, but while the nomination met with the approval of almost every one present, no attempt was made to endorse Mr. Waggener's candidacy, and eventually the bottom dropped out of this wild and visionary scheme. In fact there was never a real substantial bottom to it.

Wednesday, February 22.

On Wednesday, February 22, the populist House passed, by an almost unanimous vote, a concurrent resolution, introduced by Mr. Hair, of Kiowa County, for the removal of the State Capital to the City of Kanopolis, in Ellsworth County, the syndicate owning which had offered to erect, free of expense to the State, a building in every respect as good as the Capitol at Topeka.

THE "MAXIMUM FREIGHT BILL" PASSED.

House Bill No. 281, better known as the "Maximum Frieght Bill," was also passed on this day by the following vote: Yeas, 66; nays, none. This bill, which was a substitute for four House bills previously introduced, viz: Nos. 72, 120, 134 and 171, each proposing to regulate charges for transportation on freight on railroads operating in Kansas, was reported by the Standing Committee on Railroads, consisting of Messrs. Campbell of Stafford, Whitington, Rubel, McConkey, Howard of Shawnee, McKinnie, Benefiel of Kingman, Ryan, Rice, and Kenton. It proposed to establish maximum freight rates and one of its provisions was that three railroad commissioners should be elected by the people at the general election in November, 1893. In this form the bill passed the Dunsmore House, thus showing the confidence of the Populists in the people. The bill afterwards passed the Senate, but was rejected by the Douglass House.

A STRONG STATEMENT.

The following statement, prepared by a leading Populist editor, was given out for publication, as showing a complete justification for the attitude of the Populist party.

Now that comparative peace reigns about the State Capitol, and Republicans are clamorous in their boasting and affect to believe they have gained their point, it will be well to make inquiry and note the facts. Such inquiry will establish the fact that the Populists have never lost sight of the one great essential in this contest and come out of this imbroglio secure in its possession. That essential is the "preservation of the Populist House." To suppress this, to destroy it, to wipe it out of existence, was the dastardly and far-reaching purpose of the Republicans when they precipitated the late insurrection. Could they have accomplished the suppression of that House, they would have thwarted all possibility of any reform legislation. They know that laws passed by the assistance of that House are valid. They know that the Supreme Court that would declare otherwise would have to reverse all respectable precedent, immolate itself to the basest partisan demands, and face a wave of public indignation unparalleled since the day when the notorious Judge Tresilian was followed to the scaffold by an outraged people, where they beat him with staves to make him ascend, and then exulted at his just but shocking execution.

Corporate greed is determined to prevent the enactment of the reform measures of the Populists. No Supreme Court in these days of suspicion and imputations against the integrity of courts cares to assume that responsibility of declaring those laws void. One happy solution presented itself to the nefarious schemers, and that was the extinction and suppression of the Populist House. They did not merely intend to prevent it from meeting in Representative Hall, but they intended to prevent it from meeting anywhere—to deprive it of existence, so that no official acts could flow from it.

Their first of a series of contemplated steps to this end was the attempted arrest of the chief clerk of the Populist House. Resistance by the Populists to the execution of this Republican scheme precipitated the armed Republican insurrection.

Now that peace has been declared, it should be borne well in mind that the Populists have carried their point, and have wrung from the Republicans a solemn pledge to cease all futher attempts to molest or attempt the extinction of the Populist House. The compulsory vacation of Representative Hall may not be pleasant to the personal feelings of Populists, but it is the price Populists pay for believing that Republicans possessed a particle of loyalty or respect for law or official oaths. When the Governor found himself confronted by the Sheriff of Shawnee County and a huge horde of drunken ruffianly deputies, said to be largely from Missouri, present, he also found that the militia of the State (on whom he had to rely) were stained through with treason. The commanding officer was the first to make known his contempt for his official oath, and that he would not obey orders from his superior officer. Hence, when it is said that the Governor has made terms with a power which a short time ago he termed a lawless body, we frankly admit it, and say that he did it just as the Union men at Ft. Sumter recognized Jeff Davis, or the loyal people of Lawrence recognized Quantrell.

The disloyalty of the present militia tells the whole tale. Good Republican authorities privately admit that for the past two years the militia has been weeded out, recruited, and doctored to this end. The knowledge of this fact explains the nefarious conduct of the Shawnee County Sheriff. The Constitution of this State says:

"The Governor shall be Commander-in-Chief, and shall have power to call out the militia to execute the laws, to suppress insurrection, and to repel invasion."

But the partisan sheriff, after involving himself in evasions and gross contradictions, perceiving that the Governor was helpless in the midst of a cowardly and disloyal militia, raised an army of deputies, many of whom were the most vicious and depraved characters, filled with rum and continually talking about hanging the Populists leaders. Backed up by this motly crew, the Sheriff denies the Governor the powers conferred on him by the Constitution, and, under threat of bloodshed and an assault upon the State-House and the Governor's feeble forces, compels him to treat with the lawless and treason-infected Republican gang.

Although treating in the face of such adverse circumstances, the Populists have not surrendered one iota that is essential. So far as Representative Hall is concerned, many Populists and Populist pap.rs advised weeks ago that the Populists vacate Representative Hall and retire to where they are now going. Had they done so, Populist legislation would be much further advanced than it is now. Beyond the indignity, the vacating of Representative Hall amounts to nothing, and the unmasking of Republican treason, perjury, and general lawlessness richly compensates the Populists for all the indignities they have suffered.

What the Populists must not surrender is the Populist House. This is vital. Whether the Republicans have really abandoned their intentions to forcibly strangle the Populist House remains to be seen.

The chief reliance of the Republicans is the treason-infected militia. Kansas Republicans applauded when a Pennsylvania militiaman was hung up by the thumbs and subjected to harsh and cruel treatment because he had spoken disrespectfully of a cruel-hearted man of wealth, but now we see those same Kansas Republicans applauding

Kansas officers and privates because they violate their oath of enlistment, disobey their officers, and encourage a County Sheriff in open violation of law, backed up by a legion of cut-throat scoundrels from Kansas City, St. Joseph, and St. Louis.

The legislative proceedings of the next two days were devoid of any startling or sensational feature. Mr. Seaton's resolution for ousting the Populist members came up in the Douglass House Friday and was again postponed until 2 p. m. Saturday. Resolutions were adopted denying the right of the Governor to call out the militia and complimenting Col. J. W. F. Hughes for "his brave, wise and manly course in *refusing to obey*" the orders of his Commander-in-Chief.

"AUSTRALIAN BALLOT" BILL.

The Populist House on the same day (February 24) passed by a unanimous vote the "Australian ballot" bill," which had already been passed by the Senate, being a substitute for Senate Bills Nos. 18, 130 and 141. A like bill (House Bill No. 317), having the same title and containing the same provisions, had been introduced in the Dunsmorse House and reported favorably by the Committee on Elections, but when the Senate bill was messaged over, this House proceeded at once to consider the latter and concurred in its passage. It was subsequently passed by the Douglass House and is now in force in Kansas.

BEGINNING OF THE END.

THE SUPREME COURT REFUSES THE WRIT OF HABEAS CORPUS PRAYED FOR BY L. C. GUNN, AND DECLARES THE DOUGLASS HOUSE THE LEGAL AND CONSTITUTIONAL HOUSE OF REPRESENTATIVES—THE POPULISTS DECIDE TO SUBMIT UNDER SOLEMN PROTEST AND ENTER THE REPUBLICAN HOUSE

Interest had all week been gradually concentrating more and more on the proceedings of the Supreme Court, where the Dunn case was on trial, and when Saturday arrived, the fact that it was the day on which was to be decided the status of the republican House, was the first thing that suggested itself to the mind of the average citizen, regardless of party.

Early as was the hour announced by the court for handing down its decision, 9 o'clock, the crowd began to assemble in the corridor in front of the court room before the court officers themselves arrived to open up for the day. Clerk Brown reached his office at 8:40 and five minutes later the room was comfortably filled. The crowding and packing then began and continued until it seemed impossible that another person could find standing room in any nook or corner. The hall leading to the judges' chambers, as well as the corridor, was packed as completely as the court room itself, and scores of people were unable to obtain admission or even get within hearing distance.

Probably no such audience ever assembled before to listen to a decision of the Supreme Court of Kansas, for, in addition to its unusual size, this one comprised representatives of every political party, ladies as well as gentlemen, State officials, Senators and members of the dual House, judges and prominent attorneys from every part of the State, ministers, and, in short, men from every walk in life, and black men as well as white.

At 9:25 the Court made its appearance, Chief Justice Horton at the head, followed by Associate Justices Johnson and Allen. As they took their seats the hum of conversation almost ceased, and at the first rap on the desk absolute silence prevailed, and every eye was fixed upon the Court.

The opinion of the Court was delivered by Chief Justice Horton, slowly, clearly and distinctly. It upheld the claims of the Douglass House. At the conclusion of Judge Horton's opinion, in which Justice Johnson concurred, which was ended at 11:10 a. m., Justice Allen dissented in a strong and able opinion.

The Chief Justice announced that the court would make an order that the petitioner be remanded to the custody of the Sergeant-at-arms, and that, in accordance with the bond filed by him, he would obey its provisions and give himself up.

The one question asked on all sides when the audience broke up was, "What will the Populists do about it?' These gentlemen, one and all, expressed themselves as disposed to abide by the decision.

The Dunsmore House, upon learning that the Supreme Court had held the Douglass House to be the legal and Constitutional House of Representatives, resolved itself into a committee of the whole to consider matters pertaining to the future conduct of that body. The proceedings were held behind closed doors. Numerous and protracted caucuses took place between 1:30 p. m. Saturday and Monday evening, when, with the Governor and Senators in attendance, it was agreed to submit to the decision of the Court under the most solemn and determined protest.

At a late hour Monday night, the Dunsmore House decided to march in a body to the Hall of Representatives on Tuesday morning and take their seats in the House held by the Court to be the legal and Constitutional House of Representatives of the State of Kansas.

The Populist House did not, however, abandon its organization without placing itself on record and clearly defining the conditions under which such action was taken. Immediately after the opinion of the Court in the Gunn *habeas corpus* proceedings was handed down, Hon. J. M. Dunsmore, pursuant to a resolution to that effect, appointed a select committee to prepare an address to the Senate which should be in the nature of a protest against the remarkable decision written by Chief Justice Horton and concurred in by Associate Justice Johnson, making a majority of the members of the Supreme Court, which document was first submitted to the House, and, having been duly approved by that body, was afterwards submitted to the Senate. This was in substance as follows:

A SOLEMN PROTEST.

The people of Kansas are menaced with impending dangers of a grave character. The election of the entire state ticket, supported by the party of the people as against wrong and oppression was unquestioned. Beyond all question a majority of eight or more of the members of the house of representatives were also elected by the people's party, but the will of the people was thwarted by means of deliberate frauds perpetrated in many districts, and upon false and fraudulent returns certificates of election were issued to men not entitled thereto, while those who had received a majority of the legal votes were deprived of any right or recognition, either through canvassing boards or through the courts.

In the house of representatives there were two contending factions, one claiming to hold a majority of the certificates of election issued by the late state board of canvassers, and the other claiming to represent sixty-eight of the legally elected members of the House of Representatives. This body organized by selecting the Hon. J. M. Dunsmore as Speaker, Pen C. Rich as Chief Clerk, and Leroy F. Dick as Sergeant-at Arms.

The other party, resting its claim upon the fact that "certificates" precluded inquiry respecting either the eligibility of the holder, or whether he has been elected by legal or illegal votes, organized by choosing Hon. George L. Douglass as Speaker, Frank L. Brown as Chief Clerk, and C. C. Clevinger as Sergeant-at-Arms. Thus organized, the two bodies proceeded to go through the form of transacting business as a House of Representatives.

The Dunsmore House was duly recognized by the Senate and by the Executive of the State as the lawful House of Representatives It concurred with the Senate in the passage of bills. Bills so passed were presented to and approved by the Governor, and were duly certified by the Secretary of State, and thereafter published in the official State paper, and became laws binding alike upon all the people, and all the departments of State government. The Douglass House was not recognized as a legal department of the Government.

The Douglass House sought by means of an armed mob to dislodge the rightful House of Representatives, and to over-awe and control the other branches of the State government. They resorted to false and collusive measures to obtain a "judicial decision" in their favor. Two cases were concocted One in the Shawnee District Court, commenced by a local officer, without right or authority. in the name of "The State of Kansas," to enjoin the State Auditor and State Treasurer from paying out moneys appropriated by an act which had been duly passed by the Dunsmore House, and approved by the Governor.

An injunction against the Auditor and Treasurer as prayed for was granted. That suit or proceeding was concocted for the purpose of getting a supposed judicial recognition of the Douglass House.

The Douglass House resorted to another device to get the State Supreme Court to go outside of its constitutional jurisdiction and by means of a sham case obtain a political decision. To this end the Douglass House caused a man named L. C. Gunn to be subpœnaed to appear before its Committee on Elections in a supposed "pending contest case." Mr. Gunn refused to obey the subpœnae, and was "attached for contempt" by the Douglass House, and came to Topeka, where he commenced habeas corpus proceedings in the Supreme Court. Mr. Gunn was admitted to bail by the Supreme Court.

The Supreme Court had the right to hear and determine whether Mr. Gunn was illegally restrained from his liberty, but it had no right or authority to inquire into any political question.

But in utter disregard of all precedent and all authority under the Constitution, two of the Justices usurped a power and a jurisdiction not known to our laws, and made a decision which is not merely illegal and void for want of jurisdiction, but which is in its nature and tendency destructive of all government by the people. It is a political decision made by partisan Judges, in the exercise of powers usurped by them, and in direct violation of the fundamental principles of governement.

The situation which presents itself to the members of the Dunsmore House is this, whether in the good name of the State and the interests of the people, they will, in order to avoid a clash of arms and a contest between themselves and armed forces brought here by railroad corporations, composed of Pinkerton detectives, thugs and Deputy Sheriffs, or whether they will bow to the situation in order to secure so much as possible legislation for the protection of the people of the State, and go into or recognize the Douglass House as the House of Representatives. It is a most humiliating position for the members of the Dunsmore House, and for the people of the whole State. But something must be done, and must be done at once; and the members of the Dunsmore House, after having duly weighed and considered the vast interests which are involved in the controversy which will be determined by a submission on their part, have finally resolved that they will take their place in the House of Representatives as members thereof, and abide the consequences, trusting to the people of the State that their actions in this regard will meet their approval, and that better results will flow therefrom than from an action which shall produce greater political disturbances and strifes. But we do this under the most solemn protest, that the membership of the Dunsmore House represents a large majority of those who were honestly and fairly elected as members, that their proceedings up to the present hour have been lawful, and have been conducted in the interests of the people of the whole State. And we so sign our names to this solemn protest, and ask that the Senate shall place the same in full upon its journal.

END OF THE WAR.

THE DUAL HOUSE UNITED AT LAST—THE POPULIST REPRESENTATIVES ENTER THE HALL WITH COLORS FLYING—THEIR PROTEST PRESENTED FOR FILIND—THE SENATE PROTEST —THE WORK OF LEGISLATION PROCEEDS QUIETLY.

In obedience to the mandate of the Supreme Court, though under the triple protest of the Governor, the Senate and the members of the Dunsmore House, the Populists on Tuesday morning, February 28, took their seats in the Douglass House and for the first time addressed the presiding officer as "Mr. Speaker."

The final act by which the rival legislative bodies were merged into one, was accomplished at 10 o'clock in the forenoon, and was as remarkable a proceeding, not to say sensational, as has ever been witnessed at the Capital of any sovereign State. The Hall of Representatives was filled long before the hour of 10 arrived. The galleries were packed to suffocation. At the precise hour the Populist procession appeared at the main entrance and was admitted to the hall. Speaker Pro Tem Semple led the heroic band, followed by Sergeant-at-Arms Dick, who carried a large American flag. Then came Speaker Dunsmore and the members of the Populist House, the entire body moving down the center aisle and occupying the seats formerly appropriated by the members on the north side of the room. There was a murmur of applause from the Republican side of the House, but it was almost instantly suppressed, and there was no attempt at any demonstration from the galleries.

Speaker Douglass' gavel was heard calling the House to order, and visitors were requested to vacate the seats of the members, which they had taken possession of for several days. Clerk Brown immediately proceeded with the roll call, the Populist mem bers answering promptly and cheerfully, with now and then one rising to a question of personal privilege. Among the latter was Representative Lupfer, of Pawnee, who said he desired to enter his protest in thus being forced into the Republican House by the decision of the Supreme Court, and that on returning home he intended to have it spread throughout the length and breadth of the land, that all might know his sentiments. He had a written protest, signed by the committee of the Populist House, of which he was a member, and asked that the Clerk read it, and that it be spread upon the Journal of the House.

The Speaker said there was no rule under which such a request could be granted, but he would permit it to be done by consent of the members.

Mr. Dunsmore arose and addressing "Mr. Speaker" for the first time by his official title, referred the republicans to their own journal, which he said would show that the names of the Populist members had been called daily, and to the threat to vacate their seats, as expressed in Mr. Seaton's resolution, as proof that they were members of the House, and entitled to participate in its proceedings.

The protest tendered by Mr. Lupfer was thereupon handed to the Clerk and read by the order of the Speaker. It was as follows·

PROTEST OF THE POPULIST HOUSE.

Believing that County Clerks and other clerical officers of our election machinery have neither right nor power to subvert the will of the people as expressed at the polls; and

Believing that no legislative canvassing board or judicial authority has the power to enact laws, or the right to enforce rulings legalizing the use of lotteries in deciding election contests when the constitution expressly prohibits lotteries; and

Believing that no Supreme Court has the right or power to make members of the Legislature out of men whom the constitution expressly states are 'not proper to be chosen,' or 'qualified to be elected;' and

Believing that no man who by his statement established his legal residence outside of the State subsequent to his election has any right in law or justice to act as a member of the Legislature, and that no Supreme Court or other body has the power to make him a member; and

Believing that the Supreme Court is only a co-ordinate branch of the State government and that no co-ordinate branch has any jurisdiction over another, or legal power to coerce it; and

Believing futher that no partisan Court or other body has the power to make a legal or Constitutional House of Representatives out of illegal or unconstitutional members;

We desire to enter our solemn and emphatic protest against the usurpation of power by the Courts and the anarchistic, revolutionary and treasonable actions of the corporations and their devoted friend and ally, the Republican party, and we appeal to that Court of last resort, the people of the State of Kansas, to right the wrongs imposed upon them by their enemies and oppressors by the use of that most powerful weapon known to mankind, the ballot.

A. H. LUPFER,
J. J. McALENEY,
R. D. McCLIMAN.

Thus the thirty-ninth day of the eighth biennial session of the Kansas Legislature opened with the dissolution of the Dunsmore House, and where for thirty-eight days Kansas had a dual House of Representatives on this day and thereafter there was but one. There was little on the surface indicative of the great struggle which during the preceding active legislative days had absorbed the attention of members holding three political creeds, and representing the 125 Legislative Districts of the State.

In all, 118 members responded to their names, those recorded as absent or not voting being Helm, Hobson, Meagher, Raemer and Wright. The names of Brown and Noble, whose seats had several days previously been declared vacant on the ground of their being postmasters at the time of election, and therefore not eligible to office, were not called.

The Speaker was authorized to reorganize the list of standing committees, and at 2 p. m. the House went into Committee of the Whole for the consideration of a bill to create a uniform series of text books, in which decidly modern and prosaic manner "the war of 1893" ended.

THE SENATE PROTEST.

The Senate at its morning session adopted the following preamble and resolutions, by a vote of 21 to 8:

Be It Resolved by the Senate that

WHEREAS, We believe that at the election held in November, 1892, the electors voting at said election fairly and honestly elected a majority of the Representatives of this Legislature who were candidates on the Populist ticket, but by fraudulent, corrupt and illegal methods of certain township election officers, Boards of County Commissioners and the State Board of Canvassers, certificates were unlawfully issued to certain Republican candidates clearly not entitled to them; and

WHEREAS, This Senate believed that the will of the people as expressed at the ballot box should be upheld, and that a majority of the Representatives honestly and fairly elected by the qualified electors should be entitled to organize the House of Representatives, and that they did so by electing J. M. Dunsmore as Speaker. and Ben C. Rich as Chief Clerk. We therefore recognized said House as the proper and constitutional body with which the Senate should transact business pertaining to legislation; and

WHEREAS, The three co-ordinate branches of our State government are the Executive, Legislative and Judicial, each separate from, independent of, and in no way answerable to the other, but the Supreme Court of this State, in a partisan decision, rendered by the two Republican Judges thereof, have presumed to consider the executive and legislative branches subordinate to it, and have attempted to sustain another organization, presided over by George L. Douglass, and not recognized by the Senate or Executive, and have inferentially declared that laws enacted by the Senate, the Constitutional House of Representatives, and approved by the Executive, will be by them held invalid, thereby preventing any needed legislation for the relief of our people, and the appropriations necessary for the maintenance of our State government and the support of our educational, charitable and penal institutions.

While we recognize the right of said Court to pass upon the validity of and interpret the laws so passed, we must emphatically deny the authority of said Court to pass upon any question relating to the organization of either branch of the Legislature.

We recognize fully that there is no peaceable appeal from such unwarrantable decision, except to refer them to the power that makes Courts—the people—and knowing that our citizens are peaceable and order-loving citizens, we have determined to temporarily submit to the unjust and arbitrary exercise of judicial authority, and remand the case back to the people for their approval or rejection. Now, therefore, be it

Resolved, That the Secretary of the Senate be instructed to message the bills, joint and concurrent resolutions already passed or to be passed by us to the House of Representatives presided over by George L. Douglass as Speaker; and be it further

Resolved, That we will do all in our power to redeem our pledges to our constituents, and give them the legislation they demand, and so badly need, and should such legislation fail we will let the blame rest upon the persons responsible therefor, and place them before the bar of public opinion.

THE RESULTS.

WHAT THE POPULIST REPRESENTATIVES WON BY THEIR PLUOK, PERSISTENCE AND SUPERIOR GENERALSHIP—THE ENEMY UNMASKED AND LOCATED WHERE THEY CAN BE FOUND WHEN OCCASION REQUIRES—LEGISLATION THAT WILL BENEFIT THE PEOPLE.

It is not so long since the events to which this history relates occurred that any one should have forgotten them, yet sufficient time has elapsed to review dispassionately the greatest political conflict in the history of Kansas.. It is impossible to do so without a feeling of admiration for the marvelous patience and heroic persistence of the representatives of the people under circumstances so trying. From a tyranny less galling, e exactions less burdensome and frauds neither so barefaced nor monstrous as those suffered by the citizens of Kansas during the thirty years of almost undisputed control of the state government in all its branches by the Republican party and its corporation allies, armed revolts have sprung and empires have been overthrown.

In these three decades the state debt was enormously increased, the county and municipal indebtedness was pushed to the verge of bankruptcy, and private obligations grew to be an intolerable burden. At the same time property values and the price of farm products depreciated until the owner of real estate of any description was impoverished and the tiller of the soil was unable to realize the cost of production. The railroads became the ruling power in the state, monopolistic corporations took root and flourished on Kansas soil, the money loaner found here a fruitful field for usury and extortion, and all these enriched themselves at the expense of the agricultural classes and of the wage earner generally. Those who suffered from oppression and misrule remonstrated, but the party lash was wielded with a strong hand and they continued to vote the Republican ticket, to rivet the fetters that enslaved them and to dance to the music of their masters until the Republican majority in this state had swelled to the tremendous extent of 82,000. The party in power felt that it was invincible, and that it held a life tenure in this state, and its leaders became more arrogant, dictatorial and unscrupulous in their management of public affairs.

The people had surrendered their liberties and had seen their property rendered worthless or become so encumbered with debt that their condition was inferior to that of slaves, who at least are free from care and responsibility, and who from the self interest of their masters, are not permitted to suffer for the necessities of life. Thousands abandoned their homes and farms after years of toil, hardship and privation, and moved on toward the mountains, often without a day's food for themselves or forage for their cattle. Other thousands found themselves unable even to get out of the country, and continued to labor and to starve, that they might pay tribute to Cæsar. But they had not lost the spirit of manhood and that indomitable pluck and courage which had led them to endure the privations and trials of pioneer life, now led them to inquire as to the cause of their trouble, and having found it, to apply the remedy. The result was, to the republican party, a humiliating defeat in 1890, and utter route in 1892. It was in vain that its leaders and their corporation allies resorted to falsehood and fraud in the election and on the returning board. The people had secured control of all the State offices, elected nearly all the Congressmen, the State Senate and a majority of the House of Representatives—in short the entire machinery of the State government passed from the hands of the Republicans into the hands of the Populists, and the victory was complete.

That it was the manifest purpose of the Republican party to make the will of the people as expressed at the polls secondary to the will of the Republican party as represented by certificates of election secured by methods pregnant with fraud and corruption, has been clearly shown. Would it not have been strange indeed that a party that had elected an entire state ticket, a Supreme Judge, and a Congressman-at-Large by majorities ranging from 5,000 to 7,000, and had elected a large majority of the Congressmen and State Senators, should have failed to elect a majority of the House of Representatives? From every stand point of reason and logic, the presumption would be against such failure.

The pivotal point was the organization of the House of Representatives, because the making of laws requires the concurrent action of both Houses and the Governor, and by controlling one branch the Republicans could nullify the action of the other, and that was exactly what they were after. The people demanded certain clearly defined laws, among others one controlling the railroads and making them the servants of the people instead of their masters. The railroads, like the slaveholders of ante-bellum times, asked to be let alone. Having shaped and controlled legislation ever since their advent in the State, they were opposed to any change in the laws they had made—made to obey or not, as seemed best afterwards.

In such an emergency the People's party representatives had but one alternative. They must either quietly submit to barefaced robbery of their rights and the rights of the people by whom they had been elected, or they must resist with every lawful means at their hands. They were in honor bound to choose the latter course, and they did not hesitate, with the full knowledge that their cause was right, to assume the responsibility.

To have refused would have been to destroy the last vestige of hope for the relief of the people, and would have been an utter stultification and surrender of every principle of manhood and every right of citizenship. It would, further still, have deprived the Populists of all possibility of of proving their charges of corruption and fraud upon the part of the republicans, of conspiracy between the old dominant party and the corporations, and of demonstrating their own good faith by attempting to carry out their pledges to the people who elected them.

The Populist Representatives selected their course wisely, and in the face of the most powerful opposition completely unmasked the corporations and compelled them to show their hand in controlling and directing Republican councils.

This was one grand result of the contest which alone was worth all the risk and anxiety and labor of the undertaking. As has been aptly said by "One Who Was There," and who used substantially the same words and argument with which this chapter is opened:

"It is worth much in war to know the exact location and strength of your enemy."

The investigations of the Elections Committee of the Dunsmore House have plainly and conclusively demonstrated that the Populists legally elected at least sixty-five of the 125 members of the House. It has been shown that fraud, bribery and corruption were resorted to by the Republicans in order that the will of the people as expressed at the ballot-box might be defeated and the control of corporation power be extended for at least two years more.

The fact has been demonstrated to the world that, at the bidding of a powerful railroad corporation owned by English capitalists, the Republican party of Kansas would resort to violence, bloodshed, treason and anarchy in order to prevent reform legislation.

It is submitted to the public to decide whether or not the same railroad corporation controls the action of the Supreme Court of the State of Kansas, whose Chief Justice can one day reject the identical authority cited by himself on the preceding day in rendering a decision, and who, in defiance of all authorities, usurped a jurisdiction and power never granted him by the people, but distinctly granted by the Constitution to the Legislature.

Again, the Senate and the Dunsmore House, in spite of unprecedented and well nigh insurmountable obstacles, passed bills covering every essential demand made by the People's party in its platform, thereby showing the sincerity and good faith of the Populist leaders and the Representatives chosen by their party.

Finally, when the Governor and Legislature were compelled to recognize under protest the Douglass House, which had been galvanized into life by the usurpation of the Supreme Court, the Populists, though defeat-

ed in the main issue, railroad legislation, which had been the real cause of all the trouble, succeeded through superior skill, generalship, pluck and perseverance, in passing numerous important bills, which will materially benefit the people and assist them in their future attempts to rid themselves of British rule. Among these may be mentioned:

The Australian ballot system and the bribery law. which will make the boodle business a dangerous tool to handle.

The bill making silver a legal tender in Kansas and abrogating the gold clause in contracts, (a bill prepared by Hon. A. C. Shinn, of Franklin county, and worked through by Representative Green, of Cowley County, a gentleman of rare ability).

The mortgage redemption law.

A law reducing the penalty on delinquent taxes one-third, and reducing interest on tax sales from 24 to 15 per cent.

A bill compelling railroads to put in scales at certain points and making them liable to the shipper for shrinkage in weights on grain, seeds and hay; providing the loss is more than one-fourth of one per cent.

A quarantine law to protect the state from cholera.

An insurance law which prevents "scaling down" and compels the payment of the face of the policy in case of loss.

A bill submitting an amendment to the constitution giving woman the right of suffrage.

Prominent among the bills passed by the Populist House were the following:

An act amendatory and supplemental to the code of civil procedure in relation to sales of real property. This bill provided that "in cases where real estate, or any interest therein, sold upon execution or judicial process, where there has been no appraisement, and has not realized at such sale a fair and adequate price, the court shall, upon notice to all interested parties, and upon motion, to be filed within ninety days from the date of such sale, by the debtor or creditor, or any lien holder, or other person interested therein, or affected thereby, vacate such sale for such inadequacy of price; and upon the hearing of such motion, any of the parties thereto shall, upon demand therefor, be entitled to a jury trial upon the question of such adequacy of price.".

An act to repeal section 1 of chapter 66 of the laws of 1872, known as the waiver-of-appraisement act. This bill was in the interest of the people, and especially of the poor debtors.

An act to regulate the weighing of coal at the mines. This act was intended to protect miners, by securing to them full payment for their labor.

An act relating to the appraisement of lands, and amendatory of section 453 of the code of civil procedure. This act compelled the sheriff to cause all lands taken on execution or order of sale to be appraised by three disinterested householders, even if the contract contained the words, "appraisement waived."

An act to regulate railroads, and establish reasonable maximum charges for transportation of freight on the differnt lines of railroad in the state of Kansas, and providing for a State Board of Railroad Commissioners, with general power of supervision over the transportation lines within the State, and giving to such Commissioners full power and authority to control, fix and regulate the charges and rates; to be collected by railroad and transportation lines in Kansas, and to prevent unjust and unreasonable discrimination in such charges, and providing for the selection of such Commissioners, and the manner in which they shall be chosen, and prescribing their compensation and duties, and making appropriations to enforce this act. This bill proposed to establish maximum freight rates, as indicated by its title given above. One of the provisions was that *three Railroad Commissioners should be elected by the people at the general election in November, 1893!*

An act prohibiting railroad companies, other corporations or persons from employing or using private armed detective forces during railroad strikes or other disturbances between such companies, corporations or persons and their employes, and providing a penalty for the violation thereof.

An act to compel railroad and other assessors to assess railroad and other property at its true value in money, and providing a penalty for the violation thereof.

An act to protect counties, cities and townships against the illegal or fraudulent acts of their officers.

An act authorizing any resident tax payer to enjoin the issue of bonds about to be unlawfully issued.

An act to secure uniformity in listing and taxation of bonds, mortgages, notes and other securities.

An act providing for the weekly payment of wages in lawful money of the United States. This bill provided that "all private corporations doing business within this State shall pay to their employes the wages earned each and every week in lawful money of the United States, and all such wages shall be due and payable, and shall be paid by such corporations, not later than Saturday of each week for all such wages earned the preceding week." The bill contained ample provisions and penalties to secure its observance.

THE SUPREME COURT.

SYNOPSIS OF THE DECISIONS HANDED DOWN BY CHIEF JUSTICE HORTON AND ASSOCIATE JUSTICE ALLEN IN THE L. C. GUNN HABEAS CORPUS CASE—ENCROACHMENTS OF THE JUDICIARY ON THE LEGISLATIVE BRANCH OF THE GOVERNMENT.

Probably the most remarkable event accompanying "the late unpleasantness" was the assumption of jurisdiction by the Supreme Court in settle questions belonging wholly to the Legislature, and the usurpation of powers delegated to the Legislative bodies by the Constitution. If the right of "the highest legal tribunal in the land" to determine as to the legality of a divided House is conceded, then the Chief Justice of the Supreme Court of Kansas becomes to all intents and purposes a Dictator so far as the affairs of State are concerned, and, following out the same line of argument, the Chief Justice of Supreme Court of the United States is su perior to the President, the Senate and the National House of Representatives.

The Supreme Court of Kansas, in common with like bodies in the other States, is already clothed with a vast amount of authority. It is empowered not only to pass final judgment upon cases involving, perhaps, millions of dollars, but at its discretion it may imprison a man or set him free, and all but send him to the gallows. In short, its authority is well nigh unlimited and the only restraining power heretofore recognized is the legislature, in the make-up of which the people have been permitted to select men on whose wisdom and integrity they depended, and who would enact laws in accordance with their views on all questions. If, now, the supreme court is to pass upon the qualifications of legislators, and by reason of political bias and prejudice may confirm an insurrectionary faction in authority and enable it to defeat the will of the people by refusing to enact reform laws, then, indeed, is popular government become almost a thing of the past. The encroachments of the Courts on the rights of the people has been gradual but sure, and has at last become so noticeable as to attract the attention and excite the alarm of some of the most conservative men and deepest thinkers of the country. How this usurpation of authority may be checked is a problem that remains to be solved, but it is beyond question that its solution will be demanded before many years.

The decision of the Supreme Court of Kansas in the case referred to, involving, as it did, the legality of the Douglass House, attracted the interest of members of every party throughout the entire nation. While the criticisms of the leading newspapers of the east and west were more or less shaped by the political tendencies of their managers, the people, regardless of partisan prejudice, in their hearts, if not openly, condemned the ruling by which the Populist House of Representatives was dissolved and merged into the Douglass House. The following is a synopsis of Chief Justice Horton's opinion, in which Justice Johnson concurred:

Judge Horton's Opinion.

After briefly reciting the facts concerning the arrest of L. C. Gunn upon a warrant issued by the Douglass House, and his application to the court for a writ of habeas corpus, and reviewing the arguments advanced by counsel for the petitioner and the respondents, the court cited the law which declares that in certain cases the writ of habeas corpus would not lie, and quoted the following from the statute:

"Third—For any contempt of any court, officer or body having authority to commit."

"Therefore," said the court, "we have before us, necessary for our determination, the question whether the House which authorized the arrest and detention of Gunn had any legal or constitutional power so to do. If there were but one house to consider our duty would be plain and easy, but it appears that upon the 10th day of January two Houses met and attempted to organize, which have since attempted to act separately and independently of each other."

ORGANIZATION.

The Court then proceeded to consider the organization of these two alleged Houses, and the question of the proper method for such organization. Section 509 of McCrary on Elections was then quoted in full, being to the effect that only those holding the usual credentials of membership could be allowed to participate in the preliminary organization of a legislative body. This was followed by pertinent quotations from Cushing's Manual to the same effect, and from a late decision of the Supreme Court of Nebraska, which says:

It is contemplated that each House of the Legislature shall be organized by the persons who are *prima facie* members thereof. It requires no argument to prove the disastrous consequences of a different construction of the Constitution.

By way of illustration of the force of the Nebraska decision, the scenes which had occurred in the Kansas Capitol within the past few weeks were cited. Our own statutes, which require that the Legislature shall be constituted only of those members who hold certificates of election from the State Board of Canvassers, and detailing the routine by which those certificates shall be authorized. Obedience to these statutes has been the custom and usage in Kansas for the past thirty years, and has some of the binding force of law and evidence upon questions of this character.

A CASE FROM MAINE.

Against this view, asked the Court, what authority or reason can be brought? A case was cited from Maine in which, with a few exceptions, the Court expressed its full concurrence, wherein it was held that the returns before the State Board of Canvassers, and concerning which the advice of the Supreme Court had been asked, were better evidence of the right of members of the Legislature than the fraudulent certificates issued by the Board of Canvassers in violation of the law and the decision of the Supreme Court. In this case no such thing appears. A certificate list of the members, accompanied by a statement of the number of votes cast by each, was introduced in evidence, and while there has been much said about fraud by the Canvassing Board, there has been nothing presented in the case showing any fraud on their part.

The Rosenthal case was referred to, and the Court stated that after it was over the Chief Justice had received a letter from Mr. Rosenthal, in which he said he was convinced that "the decision of the Court was not only the law, but that it ought to be the law, and that he respected the Court for its decision."

The revised journal of the Dunsmore House was alluded to as seemingly recognizing the fact itself that only certificated members have a right to act. Wherever this universal rule has been disregarded, disturbance and violence, and almost bloodshed, have always occurred.

THE REED RULE.

The Court then said: "Then why should not, if this court has the power, say that it will recognize that House which has followed the usual and ordinary practice in convening, in Kansas."

Reference was next made to the practice of the Dunsmore House in counting as present Republicans not voting, in order to make a quorum of certificated members, and in accordance with the Reed rule and the decision of the Supreme Court of the United States upon this rule. But it was pointed out that the Dunsmore House had omitted to lay the foundation for such a practice by failing to adopt such a rule. Moreover, the persons so counted had never recognized or acted with the Dunsmore House, and were not members thereof. Speaker Reed never counted as present any

member of Congress who had refused to recognize him as Speaker.

The Court next took up the question of the organization of the two Houses—first the Douglass house, and declared that Geo. L. Douglass had been chosen as Speaker by sixty-four duly certified members. Lengthy quotations were made from the majority and minority reports of the Senate Committee on Elections in the contest cases from Montana, upon the force of the election certificates. The circumstances of the organization of the Douglass House by sixty-four members, the admission of Mr. Rosenthal, and the accession of the two Democratic members, were narrated. This gave the Douglass House an unquestionable Constitutional majority and made it the legal and Constitutional House of Representatives. This organization was perfected before either the Governor or the Senate had recognized the Dunsmore House. It is true that the Douglass House had received no such recognition, but it was a duly organized House for other than the mere purpose of legislation; it had the right to protect itself, to issue subpoenas, to do those things which pertain solely and exclusively to itself. Delays on the part of the House in communicating with the Governor or the Senate, or on the part of the Senate and the Executive in recognizing the House, would not invalidate its organization.

THE JOURNAL CONCLUSIVE.

The Douglass House having thus organized in a Constitutional manner, had the right to make a journal, and that journal is conclusive upon this Court. The Court now refers exclusively to the journal of the 10th and 11th, and not to the one that comes afterwards. The Court then took up the question of its jurisdiction to determine whether the Douglass House had the power to restrain the petitioner of his liberty, declaring that it would not take jurisdiction if it should not, but that it must take jurisdiction if it should. A long list of authorities was cited to sustain the jurisdiction of the Court, especially the case of Martin vs. Ingram, in Thirty-eighth Kansas, where it was decided that the Supreme Court had jurisdiction to compel the Governor to perform his duty, and the case arising in 1879 out of the attempt of the House of Representatives to associate with itself a larger number than 128. This House passed a law which was also passed by the Senate, signed by the Governor and published in the official paper. When that law came before the Supreme Court, it decided that the House of Representatives which attempted to pass it had no right to do so and it was wiped out of existence. Here the Supreme Court took cognizance of a matter that had passed the Legislature in the most formal manner, and yet there was no conflict between the Judiciary and the Executive or Legislative departments of the government.

It is said that the Court has no power to require by *quo warranto* into the rights of the membership of these bodies. This is true, and this Court itself has so decided, but, when this Court has the ultimate right to pass upon the legality of the acts of the Legislature, it has also the power to pass upon the legality of the organization of the Legislature.

WAS THE DOUGLASS HOUSE DESTROYED?

But it is claimed that the Douglass House has been destroyed and ousted by the recognition of the Dunsmore House. Is such a recognition final? It is admitted that if, after this recognition, the Douglass House had voluntarily departed and gone home, and the Dunsmore body with fifty-eight members had increased its members to the constitutional majority in any way it pleased, and had gone on and done business without interference, such recognition would be accepted by the Courts. But this is not the case here. The Court here adverted to the strenuous objection made in the Senate by Senators of all parties to the recognition of the Dunsmore House.

THE INJUNCTION VALID.

The Douglass House was not only legally organized, but its Journal shows that it has been doing, or attempting to do, business every day of its session. It has challenged the rightfulness of the Dunsmore House; it has challenged the action of the Governor and the Senate, and the very first act of legislation has been made the subject of an injunction in the District Court of Shawnee County, whose judgment until reversed is as valid and binding as the supreme edict of the Supreme Court of Kansas.

Not only that; this Court must take notice of all the usual and ordinary incidents that are transacted around us. Now, the Dunsmore House never had but fifty-eight legal and constitutional members, and so long as there is a legal and constitutional House carrying on business, this question of a *de facto* Legislature has not risen to that dignity of position that entitles it to the recognition of this Court. In conclusion, the Court said:

THE LEGAL HOUSE.

From all that we have said, our conclusion is that the House known as the Douglass House is the legal and constitutional House of Representative, and, being such House, it has the power to compel witnesses to attend and testify before it, and to punish for contempt any witness who refuses when properly subpoenaed.

It has been suggested that we should hesitate to give an opinion upon the constitutionality of either of these bodies because unpleasant complications might arise therefrom. It has even been suggested that the Governor and the Senate will not find their way clear to act with the legal House, and, therefore, the appropriations may fail, and all of the departments of the Government will be without funds; and, more unfortunate still, that the educational, charitable and criminal instiutions will be closed. We trust that such will not be the result.

We believe that the Governor is honest and patriotic; we believe that the Senate and the members of both these contending bodies are honest and actuated by worthy motives. We trust that there may be some way by which the House and Senate and the Governor can act together unitedly and harmoniously. The questions involved in this case are above party and partisanship. They concern the people, the State. The gravity of the situation we fully understand. Certainly no Constitutional or public question can be more solemn than the one now before us. While we deplore the occasion which compels us to hear and determine this case, we feel constrained by the imperative command of the Constitution and by the conscientious discharge of our duties, to declare our views irrespective of policy and irrespective of expediency. Justice Johnson concurs fully in the views of the Chief Justice.

"This case is brought by a citizen of this state who is restrained of his liberty by one C. C. Clevenger, claiming to act as the sergeant-at-arms of the House of Representatives. It was conceded on the hearing that if he were the sergeant-at-arms, armed with a warrant signed by the speaker of the House of Representatives, that this detention is legal. This petitioner now asks this court to discharge him from that restraint because of a want of power in the speaker, or the gentleman, who, acting as speaker, issued the warrant. Upon an inquiry so arising it became the duty of this court to pass upon the power of George L. Douglass to issue this warrant. The court in a collateral proceeding is now called on to decide a question of right between two contending bodies, each claiming to be House of Representatives of this state,—and right here I may say that the very statement of this question in connection with an admission which was made by the counsel on the part of the respondents shows the peculiarity of the position that this court takes when it assumes to determine for itself the questions that are so presented. It was conceded on the argument of this case that this court would not have the power in an action brought directly by one of these contending bodies against the other to decide and determine this controversy and to oust the wrongful body from the possession of the office of the House of Representatives and to place the rightful body in possession of the office. Then the power of this court at this juncture is but advisory, it then has no power to go into the full merits of this controversy and to decide it according to the very right of the matter. Controversies of this kind have arisen in times past, and it is to be feared that they may arise in times to come. It is necessary that the public duties should be performed; it is necessary that power should reside somewhere to speedily settle controversies arising between contending claimants to the right to exercise the duties of the House of Representatives.

Justice Allen's Dissenting Opinion.

The following is an outline of the dissenting opinion handed down by Associate Justice Allen, which has been pronounced one of the most able opinions ever written by a member of this court:

"The questions involved in this case are perhaps of greater magnitude than those which have ever been involved in any controversy heretofore occurring in this court. It involves the constitutional powers, rights and duties that are distributed by the fundamental law among the several department of the government. In our state, as in all other other states, wo have three great co-ordinate branches of government, the executive, the legislative and the judicial; each in its sphere is supreme; each is accountable to the people, and to the people alone for its acts; neither can encroach upon the powers granted to to the other; neither can perform those duties which are entrusted by the constitution to the other.

"In what I say in this case, I may premise that I speak merely from first impression. In my judgment no opportunity has been afforded to this court to fairly consider, as a court of last resort should consider, the great constitutional questions which are presented for our consideration. As stated by the chief justice, the judges of the court spent nearly the entire day of yesterday in consultation. The examination which we have been able to make since the hearing in this case of the authorities cited by the very learned and able counsel on both sides has been of the most cursory character. It must be apparent to any lawyer that the careful digesting and careful criticism of all the cases that have been decided by courts of last resort have been impracticable, impossible to be performed by the judges of this court, and what I now say, I reserve the right hereafter when I shall prepare and file an opinion in this case, to correct any error that I may make in the opinion now expressed.

QUESTIONS THE COURT'S JURISDICTION.

"Has the constitution invested this court with the power to hear and determine controversies of this character? It was conceded on the argument and in the remark of the chief justice that the constitution has not reposed that power in this court. Then I asked, can this court in a collateral action do that which it cannot in a direct proceeding? It may be said that these questions must be settled; it may be said that this court is now, in an action of which it has unquestioned jurisdiction, called upon to decide this very question. The answer to that is that this court has already been aided by a decision. We have not here before us a case of dual organization of the legislature; we have not here before us a case as in Maine, if I catch the facts of that case correctly. I have not examined it critically. We have not a case of two Houses and two Senates each claiming to constitute the legislature and that is what is necessary to make up a legislature. But we have in this case two Houses disputing each other's rights and a Senate concurring with one of these Houses. Section 1 of article 2 of the constitution read: 'The legislative power of this state shall be vested in a House of Representatives and a Senate.' Section 3 of article 1 of the constitution reads: 'The supreme executive power of the state shall be vested in a governor who shall see that the laws are faithfully executed! The statute requires the governor to do various things with reference to the matter of laws. He must when the legislature convenes, communicate to it such information as he deems necessary. He must transmit what is known as a message to the two bodies. In transmitting that message, he must of necessity ascertain what is the House of Representatives. In the very beginning of the procedure of any legislature, the governor must of necessity find and determine what body of men compose the Senate. And in the performance of that duty, the governor of the state of Kansas is responsible to the people of the state and to no one else. The constitution and the laws the people by their suffrages have vested in him the power to investigate and determine, so far as his duties are concerned, what body is the House of Representatives. It must be conceded that no duty rests on this court in the inception of the proceedings of a legislative body to inquire and determine what body is the legislature. But that duty does devolve upon the executive. We

have also another body, the state Senate, also deriving its powers from the limitations of the constitution, also deriving its powers and authority from the people who have selected the members. Upon that Senate the duty rests just as carefully as any duty that can rest upon this court. In the discharge of the duties devolving upon them, the senators are just as supreme, their rights rise just as high and no higher than the rights of the members of this court. That Senate in the discharge of its duties must communicate with the executive department of this government; it must communicate with its concurrent branch of the law-making department of this government and where there are two contending bodies, each claiming to be the House of Representatives of this state. In the very nature of things the Senate must hear and determine the question as to which of these bodies is the House of Representatives. Possibly it may be digressing somewhat from a strict consideration of the legal questions in the case and I hope I shall be pardoned for referring to the fact that I was in the Senate at the time of the discussion of the resolution recognizing the Dunsmore House of Representatives. It is my good fortune to be acquainted with many of the senators, and among them men affiliated with the republican party, lawyers of great learning and ability whose opinions are entitled to great respect. In the discussion of that resolution from the republican side, it was conceded by several of these learned and distinguished senators that if the governor of this state had recognized the Dunsmore House as the legal House of Representatives, and if that resolution should be passed by the Senate of the state of Kansas that the whole question was concluded, that that was an ultimate and final judgment and decision of the power which under the constitution and law of this state was authorized to hear and finally decided the question as to which of these conflicting bodies was the lawful House of Representatives. The opinions of these senators it seems to me are entitled to great respect. In many of the states, and under many constitutions, the higher branch of the legislative department, as usually constituted, is the court of last resort. For many years the Senate of the state of New York was the ultimate court of appeals for the determination of all law questions in that state. The House of Lords has for centuries been the highest tribunal in England for the determination of legal controversies. I do not know at this time any such tribunal exists in any of the states but when it is assumed that the Senate of this state is a body whose devision and determination may be brushed aside as though it were not, when it is assumed that the executive of this state, the representative of all the people of this state, acting within the line of his duty, acting in the exercise of his discretion as the chief of the executive department of the government is not to be respected, and his determination not only is not conclusive but is not entitled to the respect of this tribunal, I am forced to enter my dissent and non-concurrence from any such expression of opinion.

CRITICISES THE TRIAL.

"I shall not enter into an extended discussion of the facts growing out of the organization of these Houses. In my judgment, much of the evidence which was introduced on the trial of this case was wholly irrelevant, and was such as this court should not have received. As to the exact boundaries and the definite rules which should be laid down by this court for the determination of these questions, I do not desire to express any opinion, but shall reserve the whole subject for consideration when I shall file a formal opinion in the case.

"It appears from the journals of both of these Houses that a valid controversy existed, a bona fide controversy existed as to the rights of certain members to sit in that body. Much has been said by the chief justice with reference to the **right of a body after organization to determine these controversies.** I call attention to the fact that the journal of the so-called Douglass House shows that the controversy with reference to the case of Joseph Rosenthal was determined before any organization of the House, and it seems to me that when we adopt the rule that the returning board, the state board of canvassers, by the record that it makes in the office of the votes cast, by the certificates that it issues, may determine absolutely the question as to who shall constitute the House of Representatives of this state,

that we adopt a far more dangerous rule than the rule that is contended for by the other side, that the House of Representatives which shall be recognized by the executive, which shall be recognized by the Senate shall be the House, rather than that which has been created by the state returning board, if I may use the expression. Now it appears by the journal of this so-called Douglass House that at least two members of the sixty-four certificated members were ineligible to sit in the House, were just as much disqualified from taking any part in the organization of that House as though they had been alien enemies, as though they had been regular officers of the army of the United States. The constitution, which is the supreme law and to which every department of the government must bow and must yield its unquestioned and unquestioned assent, expressly says that no person holding any office under the government of the United States shall be eligible to a seat in the legislature. That, as construed by the courts of California, Nevada, of Indiana and of other states means that they are incapable of being chosen; that it is beyond the power of the people to select and make a representative of a person who holds office under the United States. It is contended also on the other side, and possibly I speak outside of the record, although I think it appears in the journal of the Dunsmore House—I have not had an opportunity to make a critical examination of those journals—but I know it is contended that one gentleman who appeared in the Douglass house who was not a resident of the state of Kansas. If so he clearly had no right to take part in the organization of the legislature. We know in the early days of the state, and in the early troubles of this state, what occurred when those who resided outside of the borders of the state undertook to take a part in the affairs of the state.

"Now, while we are considering the dangers, while we are considering these great questions which involve orderly constitutional government, we need not shut our eyes to either one side or the other. We must look at all these matters fairly in the face. It is to be assumed that all men who are entrusted with authority will act honestly and uprightly; that every legislative body ought, as they ought to; all the members on all occasions to act with due regard to their oaths of office; with due regard to the duty that is imposed upon them as such officers, and when we assume in the consideration of any case that any officer or any body of men, in the performance of any duty which devolves on them by the constitution and the laws, will act wrongfully and freudulently, when we entertain any such presumption, we are entertaining a presumption that our much-boasted system of free government is a failure. The presumption as declared by this court in very many instances is that every officer, that every body of men will act honestly and uprightly, will discharge the duty that devolves on them under the constitution and the laws, and the presumption in this case is that the executive of this state and the Senate of this state have discharged their duties fairly and honestly.

ROTESTS AGAINST OVERRULING THE GOV-
ERNOR AND SENATE.

"Now, we are called on in a collateral roceeding to overturn the action of the xecutive; to overturn the action of the enate, to overturn a legislative body of his state which has continued from the _0th day of January down to this time, and merely on a view entertained by the members of this court as to the force and effect of certain certificates as evidence of the right of members of that body to participate in its proceedings. W   ▪ asked to overturn the result of all t.... deliberations of the Senate of this state; all the deliberations of the executive of this state with reference to the legislation which has been passed. Ought this court rightly to do so? Ought this court to do so on a brief and hasty consideration of a case of this sort, in a collateral proceeding where neither of these contending bodies has a right to be heard?

Something was said by the Chief Justice with reference to the effect of the decision made by Judge Hazen of the district court of this county in determining this question. The scope and effect of that decision is simply to restrain the treasurer of this state from paying out any money under the appropriation until such time as that case can be fully tried and determined on its merits. That is the whole scope and effect of the decision and while that order is binding until it is set aside,

while there is no question as to its binding effect upon the treasurer of this state, as a decision of the question as to which of these bodies is the legal House of Representatives, I most respectfully say that I do not regard it as a final decision at all upon that question, or having the force and effect of a judicial determination of that question.

"The time given by the constitution to the legislature for the performance of its duties has nearly expired; that is, the time for which members can receive pay. We have the spectacle of an executive, a Senate and a House of Representatives working in conjunction, passing appropriation bills, passing the various beneficial legislation demanded by the people of this state. The duties of all of these bodies have been nearly all performed. It must be evident to anyone who considers the question for a moment that it will be impractical for these two bodies, the Douglass House and the Senate, to come together in such relations with each other as ta perform the functions of the legislature during this session—during the brief periop that now remains. It seems to me that the force and effect of this decision must necessarily be that this state is without legislation this winter and that such conclusion is reached by a collateral decision in this case. Did the constitution, did the framers of the constitution, did the people of this state who adopted it contemplate that after the legislature had been in session nearly its entire limit, after the governor of the state, and all of the executive departments of the state, after even the official state paper, not allied in political sentiment with either the executive or the majority of the Senate or of the House, publishing as laws the enactments of those bodies, that after all these things have occurred, did the framers of this constitution intend that this court might then step in and brush it all away as a mere phantasm, as mere nullity in a collateral proceeding? It seems to me clearly not.

"Before the Douglass House can restrain any citizen of his liberty, it must be the House of Representatives; it must be in the discharge of the functions of the House of Representatives. This warrant was issued on the thirteenth day of February. It was issued after laws had been enacted, or attempted, at least, to ɔɜ enacted by the House and the Senate and had been approved by the governor and had been published in the official state paper. They had been filed in the office of the secretary of state, had received all tho formal sanctions that the constitution requires in order to make them effective as rules of action in this state. Then this House presided over by Mr. Douglass undertakes to exercise the power of a a House of Representatives and to restrain a citizen of his liberty. The question here presented is not so much a question whether the Dunsmore House was in fact the House of Representatives, as it is a question whether the Douglass House was in fact the House of Representatives.

"How can it be said that a body of men whom the governor of this state refuses to recognize as the House of Representatives, whom the Senate refuses to recognize, whom all the executive departments of the state refuse to recognize, can be a de facto House of Representatives? How can it be said that any officer who undertakes to discharge the duties of an office, who is not regarded as such officer by any department of the government with which it seeks to do business who cannot effectually carry out any duties devolving upon him as such officer, who cannot effectively perform any act as such officer, how can it be said that he is a de facto officer? De facto means in fact; it means in the actual exercise and discharge of the duties of the office.

"Now, something has been said in reference to the right of the House of Representatives to do some things prior to its recognition, prior to any intercourse with any of the other branches of the government. It may be conceded for the purposes of this case, in my judgment, that these things may be done by the House, yet we do not have a fully organized legislature within the meaning of the constitution until we have the bodies acting in concurrence with each other. It is true they are separate and distinct in the exercise of their duties as separate Houses, but they together form the legislature of the state of Kansas. Where there are two Houses acting together as the legislature of the state of Kansas, it seems to me an absurdity to say that there can be another House of Representatives.

"When a ... nal quorum—and I might sa, ... at I fail to find in the journal o ... uglass House, (and that is the ... ouse we have to deal with ... re) I fail to find in t. journal of the Douglass House ᵤrior to the time that these other two members took their seats, even according to the showing made in this journal, I fail to find a constitutional quorum of men who were authorized to sit in the legislature. There are at least two of the sixty-four members who claim the right to participate in the organization of the House who were clearly disqualified under the constitution, whom it is admitted here were postmasters on the 31st day of December last. That leaves the House without a constitutional quorum if there be any force in that proposition. Yet, I do not take the position that a constitutional quorum must necessarily have voted in favor of the officers who were elected by the House, nor of course, do I take the position that it was incompetent for less than a constitutional quorum to adjourn from day to day.

RECOGNITION CREATES A HOUSE, HE SAYS.

"It seems to me, however, that this rule is settled from this consideration: That prior to the time of the issuing of this writ, a sufficient number of men who were recognized by their fellows as entitled to seats in the legislature were occupying seats in the Dunsmore House and voted for half a dozen laws that were enacted and received the concurrence of the Senate and the approval of the governor. That, in my judgment, made a de facto House of Representatives, and when that body of men received the recognition of all the other departments of this state it seems to me that we had then a government in fact of this state with all its parts completed. We had a government that had heads of all the executive departments; we had a Senate that had unquestioned authority; we had a House recognized by all of the departments of the government who under the constitution of this state were called upon to recognize it. It is true it had no recognition from this court, but the constitution of the state gives this court no power to inquire. The constitution gives to this court no right to inc |rɪ into any legislative body and to ꝼ

mine who are sit there, and mented upon
in so far as I .nt I have com-
these facts, in m do not properly
mented on matte The provisions
come before this a clear and ex-
of the constitutic of the legislature
plicit that each bod exclusive judge of
shall be the sole and election and qualifications of its
the election and qualifications of its
members. It is a matter with which
the judiciary has no concern. It cannot reach its hands into either of these
bodies; it cannot bring before it the
members of either of these bodies for
examination here with reference to any
matter that is pending in any election
controversy in either of those houses.

"It seems to me that most mischievous
consequences must necessarily ensue
from the position taken by the majority
of the members of this court, that the
decision by that majority is practically
the decision that the judiciary is supreme and is above both the legislature
and the executive.

"I have no criticism to make on the
suggestion that it is the duty of the
judiciary to determine wherein the law-
making power may have transcended its
authority in the passage of laws. I
have no question that this tribunal may
say to the legislature or to the
governor, 'you have overstepped the
boundaries of your power as defined by
the constitution of this state.' But this
court has no power to go behind the authority of these bodies to act, as
such bodies and to say to any
body of men that is acting as a House
of Representatives in conjunction
with the other departments of the government, 'You are not a department of
the government; you are an interloper.'
It is not right to step in
when three branches of this government concur in the transaction of
business of this state and say, 'We will
withdraw from this government one of
its constituent parts and thereby make
the whole structure tumble to its fall:
we will thereby destroy all that you have
builded up.'

"For these reasons, and for others, I
am forced, though with much hesitancy,
and though with great dislike to do so,
to dissent, and to radically dissent, from
the views entertained by the majority of
this court."

The quiet acquiescence, under protest, of
the Populists in the decision of the majority
of the Court has already been set forth, and
as well as the avoidance of an open

conflict with the Republican House and the
mob that backed it, at once stamp as false
all charges against the People's party as an
organization whose members desire to set
the law at naught and antagonize good
government. As has already been said, the
patience of the people's representatives during the trying times of the organization of
the House and the sessions of rival bodies
in the same Legislative chamber; their
refusal to become embroiled with their
political opponents, or to furnish the slightest pretext for violence and bloodshed; their
devotion to the interests, not only of their
immediate supporters, but of the whole
people, as shown by the character of the laws
enacted by the Dunsmore house, or through
the influence of its members in the consoli-
dated house, must stand forever to their
credit as peaceable, law-abiding, order-loving
and patriotic citizens of Kansas. It is possible that partisan feeling may for a time
blind the eyes of a few to this fact, but with
the lapse of time the Populist House of
Representatives of 1893 will win the endorsement of more and more of the citizens of
this commonwealth and history will pay full
tribute to their loyalty and their fidelity to
the trust reposed in them as the people's
representatives.

One fact more may be noticed in closing,
and that is that the prophecies of the enemies of the People's party of the disaster
that would result from placing the State
Government in their hands have one and all
been utterly confounded. The various departments of state, in efficient hands, are
moving smoothly, many reforms calculated to permanently benefit all
the people have been inaugurated,
and, in short, the record of the new Administration up to the present time has in
point of excellence been unexcelled by its
Republican predecessors at any period of
the State's history.

Governor Lewelling and his associates
have become known throughout the West
and South by reason of their advanced
ideas on questions of public interest,
their courage, zeal and tireless en-
ergy, and wherever known they have won
the respect of men who are shaping the
destinies of other great commonwealths,
and who endorse the methods and plans inaugurated by the first people's party administration in this republic.

It may, with confidence, be said that
we are as yet but in the dawning of the new
era from which so much is hoped for and expected. The full glory of the day will be
realized by steadfastly adhering to those
principles which have brought about the
changes of the past four years.

The motto on Kansas' coat of arms, "Ad
Astra Per Aspera," is being realized at
last. The worst difficulties have been over-
come and the reward is within the reach of
those who have earned it. It remains but to
reap it.